# THE HUNTINGFIELD PAINTRESS

PAMELA HOLMES

BLOODHOUND
— BOOKS —

Print ISBN 978-1-914614-03-3

## ALSO BY PAMELA HOLMES

Wyld Dreamers

*In memory of my mother, Ann*

# 1

1848 AUTUMN

She steps down from the carriage into the yard. Behind the snort of horses and whispers of wind, there is silence.

It clings to the branches of the trees, hides in the hedges and the nooks of walls, seeping out again when the murmured words between her husband William Holland and the coachman cease. Moonlight spills down between broken clouds. There is the Rectory, their new home. No welcoming light at a window, only a lantern hanging by a closed front door. And over there the church, the purpose of their life here, silhouetted against the sky, headstones set round it like crooked teeth.

William takes her hand and gives an exaggerated bow.

'Your new home, my love. We are here, at last, in Huntingfield. But your hand is cold! Let's get inside.'

The front door opens and a housemaid, seemingly too shy to speak, nods at the floor. They follow her along a dim hallway and into a room rosy-lit by fire.

'Ah, a cheerful room, don't you agree? Your hat, Millie, let me lay it here. Come and sit here on the sofa. Fetch some tea, will you?' William asks.

They have waited for this day for so long that now it is here she feels deflated, unsure what to do next. She sinks back into the cushions. William draws his chair up beside her, tucks her skirts round her legs, rubs her fingers. At last the maid rattles in with a tray.

'You are Rose, I presume?'

'Yes Ma'am.'

'And Cook is ...?'

'Asleep Ma'am.'

'I see,' replies Mildred, although her tone suggests she does not.

William reaches for the teapot. 'Leave it Rose. I'll pour.'

The girl backs out of the room. A whisper of footsteps and the house is quiet again.

William raises his eyebrows. 'We're strangers Millie. She'll be wondering about her new employers, what we'll be like to work for. She'll get to know us soon enough.'

That night as she lies in the unfamiliar bed, her legs wrapped around her husband, she senses the silence pressing at the window, slithering across the floor, up the bed legs, spreading out over their bodies, pressing down, heavy, as she slides into sleep.

She knows exactly where she is. Although it is still dark, she can make out William's head by the bedside; he is praying. When she married him some thirteen years ago, he had pale brown hair; but now it is as though over-washing has drained it of colour and strength. Wispy and white, it dances in the draughts.

She waits until he is struggling to his feet, then stretches out her hand to stroke his scalp. It is one of their signs. He smiles as he clambers on to the high bed and lays down over her like a heavy sheet.

∾

'They were late in last night, Rose, past midnight? Move yourself along, will you.'

Cook, thin as a switch, riddled the range. A puff of coal-ash settled on Rose's boot. Pressed against the familiar body of the stove, Rose yawned and plaited her hair.

'They were awake early. I heard them when I came down this morning.' She did not mention the odd sounds coming from the Hollands' bedroom.

Cook set the kettle on the hot plate; it hissed crossly.

'How were they, then, our new master and his mistress?' Cook kneaded a soft mound of dough, puffs of flour dusting her eyebrows as she worked. A satisfying yeasty smell filled the kitchen. 'Pass me those bread tins, will you?'

'He's tall and she only comes up to his chest and ...'

'Not that, you great ninny. I mean, did they seem friendly or stuck up or ...?'

'Seemed all right. The Rector went to pour the tea.'

'Did he now?' Cook punched the shaped dough with her fists down into two loaf tins and slid them to the back of the range. 'Cover them with a towel, will you? So not like our last Master, Mr Uthoff? He was a piece, expecting all the women to run round after him.'

'Or hard to please like Mrs Uthoff.' As Rose poured boiling water into the teapot, she remembered the humiliation of being slapped by her previous mistress and then shouted at to stop her tears. 'I only saw 'em for a short while last night. I'm a bit worried, though.'

'That's nothing new, Rose. If there's anything to tussle over, you'll find it. Get on with yer breakfast. That bell'll be busy soon. They'll want breakfast and to see round the place. Nothing's been done in that church for years, ever since the Uthoffs agreed to sell the living. You've been here, what, six years, Rose? I'd say the Hollands waited more than eight years to take over Huntingfield. Do they know what state the church is in?'

A dismal sense of damp filled her nostrils as Mildred pushed open the door of St Mary the Virgin church. In the entrance, she waited for her eyes to adjust to the dark. Air was cold on her cheek and a regular dripping sound echoed from somewhere. A trickle of anxiety ran through her. This was the place that she and William had dreamed of all the years they lived abroad. Wherever they were – on the white-cobbled pavements of Lisbon or crossing a mountain stream in Germany – this church and the life they would build around it had always been foremost in their thoughts. Everything they saw or experienced was examined for its possible contribution to their future as the Rector of Huntingfield and his wife. When their life would start, William would always say. An invisible string tethered their hearts and minds and souls to this little stone building.

They knew something of the history of the church and the land on which it stood. That the Saxons had built a simple timber structure which rot or riots had later destroyed. That the Normans had established a small flint and stone chapel for their tenants which subsequent landowners had extended. That the building had suffered in the Reformation, like so many in the county, stripped of decoration or ornamentation. More recently, from sporadic correspondence with the incumbent Rector, Mr Henry Uthoff, they had read between the lines and understood that the building had been neglected over many years. Hints that William and Mildred might 'find it necessary to consider repairs' when they took up the living.

But she had not expected it to be in such a sorry state! The windows boarded, the walls rain-stained, the air dead. Mildred felt humiliated. Was it for this that she and William had waited all those years?

'Millie, are you there? I've brought a lamp. The stableman said the place was dark on a winter's day and he was right.'

William emerged from the gloom, his hair shining like a halo around his rotund face. He was not a handsome man. His pale skin scoured easily in the wind or sun, making red scaly patches on his cheeks; and though his height meant he could carry his increasing girth easily enough, he could not be described as nimble. But here was a kind person; his face glowed, even at rest, and his gentle eyes showed his goodwill towards the world. It made him, for her at least, good-looking in the best sense of the word.

'The church is in a terrible state, William. Such disrepair! Henry Uthoff spent money here, did he not, but where, please? I can't see that anything has been done for years. There's rain getting in, I can smell damp. To call it plain and simple would suggest someone has given it a moment's thought, and that is clearly not the case. Does the Bishop know? Is it any wonder that the congregation has dwindled?'

William took her arm and they trailed down the aisle past rows of simple wooden stools and boxes where, they presumed, the congregation was invited to sit for services. Clouds of dust and dirt puffed around their legs as they made their way towards the wooden table which appeared to serve as an altar. The piece of material stretched out along it was stained and torn. The window above the altar grudgingly admitted smeared winter light which revealed engravings set into the walls, shrouded figures on one side and a marble memorial on the other.

'My dear, I don't know what to say. This is not what I expected at all. It is such a forlorn place.' He paused for a few moments. 'More neglected than I imagined. I am sorry.'

They looked back down the church. The lamplight could not penetrate much of the gloom, but it felt unlikely there was much else to see.

'But it is *our* church, Millie. Ours to cherish and to love. And we can make it a beautiful place once again. Of that I am sure.'

Just like William to be positive! She squeezed his arm and they pressed themselves together in the chill, remembering the years that led up to this point.

Being the Rector of Huntingfield was a dream William had held since he was ordained at Oxford in his early twenties. A wealthy relative had generously bought him the parish living. But as was the custom and practice, the incumbent Henry Uthoff was entitled to remain as the Rector of Huntingfield for as long as he chose. William must bide his time and take up his position only when Mr Uthoff chose to vacate the property.

'Or when his Maker calls for him.' Mildred often tried to shock her older sister, Elizabeth. They were embroidering Mildred's initials on handkerchiefs and other items for her wedding trousseau. The sisters sat by their parents' fireside in the Lincolnshire farmhouse where they had grown up, gossiping about Mildred's future.

'Whatever happens, do let's hope Mr Uthoff does not hurry away from Huntingfield too quickly, Elizabeth. I am keen to marry William, of course I am. He is the kindest and cleverest man I have ever met, and I love him very much. But I don't want to be tucked away in a quiet village being a good rector's wife too soon.' Mildred's curls bounced as she laughed. 'I am only twenty, after all. Too young to live in a village with one shop, one public house and a forge! Oh, Elizabeth, what will I do there? I'll be so lonely. I won't have you, my dearest sister, to giggle with!'

'Do you think I should warn William about the woman he is marrying?' Elizabeth teased. 'Does he really know you so well? As your older sister, let me give you some advice.'

Elizabeth took her sister's hand and gave her a serious look that was only partly in jest. 'You're marrying a churchman, Mildred, a man who will one day be the Rector of Huntingfield. That means you must support him and his parish work. You must run the household, organise the servants, and visit the sick and so on. You might even help William with his sermons. I know you will be a credit to your husband, my dear sister,' she said confidently. 'No more talk of boring Suffolk villages. It will be your life. Didn't you say there is large house nearby, Heveningham Hall? I am sure you will be invited there from time to time. And there will be other likely people in the village and round about. Cards and conversation; that sort of thing.'

The girls burst out laughing.

'Now that is something I *will* look forward to!' Mildred did a mock curtsey for her sister. 'No, Elizabeth. I must experience some excitement before I become a respectable rector's wife.'

So when it had become apparent to the young married couple and their families that they would have to wait some years before Mr Uthoff finally vacated Huntingfield, Mildred found in her father-in-law Augustus an unwitting ally. For it was his view that the annuity, which William's uncle had settled on him, would be better spent living on the Continent than going to the trouble and expense of setting up a temporary home in England. Augustus assured William that the couple could live inexpensively abroad.

'How clever of you, my dearest father-in-law!' Mildred threw her arms around Augustus's neck, startling him with a kiss. Both Holland men were unfamiliar with physical enthusiasm but surprised to find it infectious. 'William, we must listen to your wise father. And just think how exciting our life will be!'

For the idea of travelling in Europe made Mildred's eyes widen. This was a life she had never considered might be hers.

Sailing on boats, visiting museums, meeting interesting people; the prospect was thrilling.

'And of course, my dearest,' she added hurriedly, 'more importantly, we will be preparing for our life's work in Huntingfield. Do you not see this proposal is pragmatic and sensible ... and terribly exciting?'

Mildred was hard to resist and William was persuaded. For he had always harboured a fear he was considered a dull young man. At Oxford University, he had joined a group of like-minded men, the Oxford Movement, galvanised by their belief that the English parish congregations were dwindling because the Church failed to inspire religious fervour. Song and prayer would bring the people to their knees, they argued, while restoring splendour, pomp and ritual in churches would galvanise those stunted souls towards a greater love of God. William became a passionate advocate for a medieval revival in the Church of England. It also gained him the reputation for being a radical, an attribute he was secretly thrilled to learn one day from an acquaintance.

Mildred became an ardent supporter of her husband's view – who could quarrel with a belief in beauty, after all? And if travelling on the Continent was necessary for her husband's work, she would support him in that, too!

'William, think how much we will discover and learn, and then use when we finally settle in Huntingfield,' she coaxed. 'So much for us to discover. It will help in our future work in the parish if we can see for ourselves how God is celebrated and worshipped where rationalism and puritan thinking has not dominated.'

So William and Mildred joined the flow of young men and fewer women who went to the Continent on a Grand Tour. Not to dance, flirt or find a marriage partner; for them it was a chance for serious study of what they could learn and then bring back to the parish and parishioners of Huntingfield. William emphasised the serious nature of their travel to anyone who cared to listen.

'We are modest travellers,' William explained to a couple they met in Dresden when collecting tickets for the evening's performance at the Semperoper. The couples had agreed to meet for *sachertorte* at Coffee Baum afterwards.

'We've found some marvellous places to stay, haven't we William?' Mildred said. 'I must say this cake is the most delicious confection I have ...'

'Yes, but always simple, somewhere to lay a weary head,' William interrupted. 'Our work is to visit churches where I can record details of architectural features, adornments and so on. These notes will be used as ideas for the improvements we will make to our parish church when we return home. My wife helps me. She is an artist, an amateur perhaps, but very good at capturing the use of colour, pattern and styles in religious iconography.'

'You are an artist?' the man asked.

'No, William flatters me. I only sketch a little as an aide-memoire. Could I order another piece, William? The pastry here is so good. And so, where are you going to visit next?'

Later as they walked back to their rooms, admiring the flamboyant architecture of the opera house, Mildred took William's arm.

'I sometimes wonder, William, if you do not feel a little guilty that we are enjoying ourselves so much? Is that the case, my love?'

William kissed her forehead and said nothing. But eight years later, standing in their damp, dilapidated church, he found the words that sometimes eluded him. His voice echoed around the church as though addressing a congregation.

'Now we are in Huntingfield, Millie, the purpose of our

studies will be revealed. Together we will work as hard as heart and soul allow to make St Mary the Virgin worthy of our worship of the Lord. And we will bring the congregation of Huntingfield to God!'

'Yes, that is what we will do.' Mildred sounded convinced. But in her heart she knew that while for William the next steps were clear, for her the way forward was less certain.

## 2

1848 TEN DAYS LATER

The next few days were filled with sorting and unpacking. Many of their belongings had arrived several days earlier. There was linen to fold, crockery to wash, lamps to set. Mildred supervised it all cheerfully. In the last eight years she had spent little time on domestic detail. Now she was pleased to be the mistress of her own house, and she set about planning the smooth domestic function of the Rectory, leaving William free to work.

Seventeen-year-old Rose Goody almost scuppered her good intentions. The servant was so awkward that she hung her head when spoken to; Mildred saw only her pale white parting and dangling dark plaits. Rose had a Suffolk accent which made it difficult for Mildred to understand what the girl was asking. Communication with Cook was more straightforward. Mildred told her she would take little interest in how the kitchen was run; Mildred simply expected plentiful and varied meals. Cook must sort out the purchases and deal with the tradesmen.

William had insisted a third servant was needed. He engaged Thomas, the son of Robert the stableman, as houseboy to carry wood and water, clear out the fireplaces and run errands. Each morning when Thomas arrived for work, the twelve-year-old's round face and tangled hair were cheering, and the boy brought stories and gossip from the village which made them both laugh. William and Mildred insisted Thomas should not miss out on his education, so William would give the boy reading and writing lessons each day.

It was with these servants that Mildred ran the Rectory. Grand when viewed from the lane, the large house had the oddest arrangement of rooms, the result of previous owners' aspirations of grandeur coupled with haphazard building, Mildred decided. There was an elegant high-ceilinged drawing room at the back of the house with French doors which opened out to a lawn and a pond with a little bridge. Next to the drawing room and down a narrow set of stairs, was the kitchen and scullery. But the dining room was inconveniently at the front of the house so the servants had to run if the food was to be kept hot. Part way along the black-and-white tiled corridor connecting these two was her favourite room, the small parlour where they'd sat the first night. With its cosy fire and bay window giving a view of the church, it was William's study.

Upstairs there were three bedrooms and a fourth smaller room which William planned to convert into a bathroom. In a few months' time, he told her there would be fresh piped water, raised into the house by a pump installed in the back yard which Thomas would work each day. Also, there would be a water closet that flushed fresh water, a device William had seen at the Great Exhibition. Just like my William to be interested in the latest mechanical devices, she smiled to herself. What's wrong with Thomas emptying the privy?

Mildred decided the big room which looked out over the front yard would be their bedroom. Seven huge yew trees separated the Rectory from the fields which surrounded it; their sentry-like shape made her feel protected. Over their dark heads, she could see the long winding drive which led from the Rectory down to the lane. Half a mile away and out of sight was the village of Huntingfield. From her cushioned window seat, all she could see were small rounded hills, hedgerows and a big open sky.

For some days, she had avoided the upper floor of the house. William had said there were only storerooms for unwanted furniture and the servants' quarters up there. But one day after lunch when the sounds of gentle snoring from William's study confirmed her husband was 'working', she decided to explore. The hard morning frost had melted in the sunlight and the house felt chilly. Wind swirled around the house. Mildred felt uneasy. Seeing the last part of her new home would make her feel more settled, she decided.

There was no window on the back staircase. So it was hard to see where to put her foot as she carefully felt for the next wooden step up. She ascended on to a small landing; several doors led off it. This room must be where Rose sleeps, thought Mildred as she peeked in. It was small with a narrow iron bedstead, a washstand and a bowl. A rumpled mat was strewn over the floorboards. Through the open curtains dull light revealed a bedside table where a seaside postcard was propped against a china mug; a pile of white stones and two blue hair ribbons were laid in a careful line.

Sweet touches, Mildred smiled. Is Rose happy in her work? Mildred supposed Rose might harbour hopes of marriage and children one day but finding a suitable young man with a sufficient wage to support a wife and family would prove difficult in this isolated place. Perhaps she doesn't mind that much, thought Mildred, as she walked past what must be Cook's room, for two small aprons hung on the door.

In another room, Mildred saw her suitcases and some boxes stacked in tidy piles. There was only one room left for her to see.

Its closed door seemed to suggest it would prefer to remain that way. Mildred straightened her shoulders. Why didn't I bring a lamp? She scolded herself, as she reached for the handle.

It was solid. Using both hands, she twisted it hard, felt the blood pulse in her ears as she struggled. Some part of her hoped that the handle would not give but it did not stop her fighting against its resistance. Then suddenly the handle turned, the latch clicked and the door swung open. Mildred stood in the doorway, her heart still racing from her efforts. A low-eaved room stretched away; at the far end, she saw there was a barred window. Afternoon light slipped finger-like through the rents of limp curtains. A bookshelf of cobwebs and a wooden bench were pushed against the wall. The air was still.

It was as though the children had left only a moment ago. It was a sense, a smell, a presence that could not be denied. Children had been in this room; drawn and dreamed, cried and crawled. Their lives had a left a mark so strong that the air was rich with their murmurings and mutterings. It was as though they had just slipped away.

She crouched down, feeling nauseous. Saliva filled her mouth. Then she noticed it, under the bench, a tiny silver rattle with a white bone handle, hidden in the dust. It must have lain in this room soundless for years. She stretched out to rescue the ornament, curled her fingers around it, and brought it into the sunlight. Childish fingers had once made these bells tinkle. She pressed the cold metal to her lips and a surge of bile washed her teeth.

Her eyes searched for the children and her ears strained to hear their voices but she knew she would not find them. She lay herself prone along the floor, her thighs pressing into the bare boards. And now it was as if she was floating above her prostrate form, abandoned on the nursery floor like a toy. She watched as each howl started in her belly, filled her chest and poured out of her mouth. Cradling her head on her arm, tears dripped in thick plops on to the floor, making pools in the dust.

How long she lay there on the nursery floor she did not know. But at some point, she became conscious of the faint smell of vinegar and sweat. A pair of boots, scuffed and turned up at the toes, swam into view.

'Mrs Holland, what's the matter, Ma'am?' Rose squatted down; her knees cracked like a gunshot. 'Shall I call the Rector?' There was no response. She touched Mildred on the shoulder, then stood up and backed out of the room. 'I'll get the Rector,' she said firmly. The sounds of her footsteps faded as she ran down the corridor.

# 3

1849 FEBRUARY

Dear Elizabeth,
        You ask about our life in Huntingfield. We wake at six when Rose brings tea. Before breakfast, William says prayers and then we plan the day. It does not take us long for there is little variation in our daily round. William does home visits all morning or takes a baptism or marriage. I will walk unless the weather is poor and go parish visiting. At one o'clock we lunch. William takes a short nap before working in his study. He gives our houseboy his daily lesson. At six o'clock, there are evening prayers in the church. After that, we have supper on a tray, write letters and read until we go to bed about ten.

        On Sundays, we ring the changes! Holy Communion starts at eight in the morning, then there are Morning Prayers at ten and Evening prayers at six p.m. We may take a walk together after lunch. And then early to bed.

        Once a week, William holds what he calls a 'cottage' lecture. He gives one of the villagers a shilling to pay for the cost of an evening's light and fire in their cottage. He says as many as twenty gather to sing hymns and to talk. William will not invite me. With so many crammed into a small place, it can become odorous. He does not *mention it but I suspect some of the men have been drinking and he fears I will be offended.*

*As you know, Elizabeth, I am hard to offend but my kind husband does not accept this. I sit at home and sew. Sometimes I prick my finger, just to make myself jump.*

*We are happy enough here, dear Elizabeth. William says there will be more society in the summer so I wait with interest and hope! Perhaps you will come to visit when Father's health improves?*

*Your loving sister, Mildred*

While they lived abroad, she had known Huntingfield was always at the forefront of William's mind. He would repeatedly remind her of his calling. Once he stopped her, the heat of the sun pounding down on their heads, telling her urgently of how much he longed to live among 'his' people, to bring the word of God into their lives. She was transfixed by his passion, made almost inert by his energy. Only when he entered the Church could she rouse herself to follow him into the relief of the dark and the cool.

In the Apostolic Palace in the Vatican, he had lingered by the Disputation of the Sacrament, almost breathless, holding her arm. 'Look up, Millie, look up! Raphael, he shows it in paint! A physical manifestation of the glory of God. The triumph of the Church in heaven over the faithless on earth. And we, in our parish my darling, will be part of that triumph. We will bring people back to God.'

The fresco transfixed William. It was not the same for her. For Mildred, the painting was an exquisite work of art – thrilling and moving – but she appreciated it within a life that was rich with many sights, sensations and sounds. She loved even the stinks that assailed her nose! One day she must be content to sew before a fire and to raise a family perhaps; to undertake willingly the responsibilities of being a vicar's wife living in a small Suffolk village. She was confident that she would accept her lot. But until that day arrived, she wanted to see it all – looking and learning, breathing and being.

For Mildred thrived on a constant feature of their new life – change. The pair began their travels in Paris, finding a delightful apartment off the Rue de Passy. They became a familiar sight in the Notre Dame; the odd English couple often to be seen perched on travelling stools in the darker recesses of a cathedral, wrapped in rugs, drawing and writing notes about the Gothic architecture. When the weather turned wet, they left for Spain. But the flies in Cordoba irritated, so they headed down to the coast to spend several pleasant months by the sea until the heat passed. And so they wandered, guided by their faithful Baedeker or the recommendations of a fellow traveller or 'simply whim'. They visited most of Europe, lodging in small hotels or renting an apartment. They would hire a maid, follow up any introductions they had and start to work again. Italy, Bohemia, Moravia, Germany, Czechoslovakia; in Constantinople they stayed for several months. But as William said: 'we always think of Huntingfield; how we would use what we saw and what we learnt for our life's work in the parish.'

She knew also that the experience affected them both in other, more fundamental ways. It went beyond gathering knowledge and learning. She knew, even if he did not, that he was changed utterly by what he had done and seen. Hot sun on skin, the smell of lavender hills, the taste of garlic, the sound of goat bells in the mountain. Unfamiliar cultures and customs. Travelling over mountains and through deserts, riding rivers and sailing seas, it opened parts of themselves which England had never touched. William changed; no longer the stiff pompous boy who had walked the stone rooms of Oxford, he had melted into a man. Was it the smooth marble statues which released in him the drive to explore her warm flesh and blood, those dark places of pleasure with unexpected delicacy and desire? She too was different from the girl who had accepted his ring at the altar. New sensations and experiences had been ingested greedily. And these had not passed through either of them like so much digested food. The experiences lingered; made marks that went beyond memory, became bound to sinew and soul.

The postman's knock cracked the silence of the Rectory like an egg broken on a bowl. It made Rose jump, and she hurried up the steps from the kitchen. Mrs Holland was already standing at the open front door beaming, in her arms a bundle of letters, a large parcel at her feet.

'Take this, Rose, I've got the rest. Oh, marvellous, it's come early today!' She sighed happily. 'Bring the tea into the study, will you? William, are you ...?' And Mildred hurried past, flattening Rose against the wall, and went down into the study, kicking the door shut with her shoe.

Not sure why she gets so bothered up, thought Rose, drifting back to the kitchen. Cook's made a nice fruit cake and fresh scones. She's got them lovely clothes and her husband is kind.

But Mrs Holland hardly notices anything once her nose is buried in her post. Rose carried the tray into the study, quiet except for the Rector's mutterings.

'Pour will you, Rose?' he said over his shoulder. 'I must choose tonight's reading, service begins in an hour. You are coming tonight I trust?'

'Yes sir.' Rose knew it shouldn't but her heart sank. Her faith fluctuated with the temperature and at present, it was so cold in the church.

'Well if you are, Rose, go upstairs and take a pair of my wool stockings out of my mending basket. It will be chilly and you've bare legs. Some new ones have come for me today. Look, William, lovely patterns on them!' cried Mildred, waving a pair at her husband's back.

Rose could feel her cheeks reddening. Talk of stockings in the presence of the Rector made her uncomfortable.

'You're like a child at Christmas, Mildred Holland!'

Rose said: 'Should I fetch 'em stockings for down here, Ma'am?'

'What? Don't be silly Rose, I mean the stockings for you, of course. Put them on and be ready in time for the service; mend them later. There's some black garters in my wardrobe. Go on now, I will pour. William, here's your cup and your journal and a letter from I'm not sure who ...'

Upstairs in Mrs Holland's bedroom, Rose dug around the mending basket and found a pair of wool stockings. She rubbed the smooth material, smiling. Was it cheeky to put them on here, where it was warm, rather than in her freezing cold room? Leaning against the bed, she quickly drew the soft material up over her bare legs and fastened the stockings at her knee with a garter. They were soft and warm. She re-laced her shoes, another gift from Mrs Holland. Cook would be jealous, she knew, when she saw Rose had been given something else, but Cook had such a skinny frame that nothing belonging to Mrs Holland fitted her except bonnets and gloves. Rose caught sight of herself in the mirror, saw with a flash of pleasure that her calves looked trim. Mrs Holland's cream shawl lay draped over the bed frame. As quick as a snake, she gathered the soft cloud of material and wrapped it around her waist; it fell into extravagant folds and she admired herself. Like the wedding dress I'll marry in one day, she mouthed, pinching her cheeks to make them flush. Hurriedly, she straightened the quilt where she'd pressed against it and skipped back downstairs.

'You can't take them,' she heard the Rector grumble.

'But I want them with me! I promise to sit on them during the service and listen to every word that you say. My letters will be flatter than the handkerchiefs Rose irons.'

'Silly Millie ... Very well, it's time to leave. Are we not expecting Thomas as well?'

Rose fixed her eyes on the pool of light cast by the Rector's lantern as she and Thomas followed the Hollands across the graveyard. It was colder and darker inside the church than outside, she thought as she settled on a bench below the altar, and she was glad of the new stockings and Thomas's warmth as he sat pressed up against her. The guttering candlelight barely illuminated the Rector's face as he started to read from the Bible. Despite the cold, Rose felt herself nod off. She hoped her employers did not see Thomas dig her in the ribs to jolt her awake.

He knew how to cheer her up. 'Mrs Holland and I will take supper in our room tonight, Rose. Make sure it's warm in there, will you? Put plenty of wood on the fire.'

It was a habit they had developed in Switzerland one evening after a long day's walk in the mountains around Wengen. What they now called their 'supine alpine' evenings. Supper in the bedroom, good things to eat and drink and Mildred propped up with pillows at one end of the bed while he massaged what she lamented were her 'fat little toes'. The candlelight picking out the colours in his whisky as he offered her little sips like consecrated wine. And they would lie together in a rosy haze, the world held at bay, social convention and expectation sunk with the sun. Sometimes the evenings were livelier when she would entertain him with stories. Mildred was a fair mimic.

'A travelling man knocked at the back door with his smooth patter and bag of tricks. I was in the drawing room and could overhear it all. He had Rose giggling, asked about "her sweetheart", her "lucky man", as quick as could be. Oh sir, you flatter me, minced Rose, there is no one special for me. Then the scoundrel sold her a bottle of his special potion. Guaranteed to warm the heart of a reluctant suitor, he promised. But William, what will her sister Mary say when Rose goes home on Sunday with a brown bottle of sugar water?'

But tonight Mildred was quiet. She lay back against the pillows, eyes half-closed, and shook her head when he offered her food he had cut into mouth-sized portions. A glass of wine on the bedside table lay untouched. William started to read aloud an article he was sure would interest her, but after a few paragraphs he set the journal down.

'What is it, my dear? You aren't listening, are you? And why aren't you eating?'

'It's nothing, William, I am low tonight, ignore me. It's cold here, such a draughty house.'

'Let me tuck you in a bit more, Millie. And build up the fire...'

'No, leave it, William, don't fuss. I'm fine ...'

'But you're not, you're not. But why? We are home at last in Huntingfield, where we have always dreamed of being. Mildred ...?'

She looked at him, and said nothing.

∾

A brick wall surrounded the Rectory garden, separating it from the woods which seemed to press right up against it. The wall was covered in roses and honeysuckle, fat buds and pale green growth suggesting spring would soon arrive. Mildred was relieved. On one side of the lawn, William planned a bowling green and talked about parties they would have in the summer. She saw where the gardener had seeded the ground and stretched lengths of string between sticks to stop the birds feeding on the early shoots of grass.

She wandered into the conservatory. Here were pots of young lemon and orange tree shoots, grown from seeds they had brought back from Italy. They put her in mind of a citrus grove she and William had visited near Naples. William, standing with a pot of water in one hand and an umbrella in the other, shading her from the sun while she did a watercolour of the fruit trees, loose smudges of orange and green and yellow. It must be in one of her sketchbooks still to arrive from storage. It was then she heard the faint ring of the doorbell and the sounds of men calling out. Unexpected visitors? She found herself hurrying back to the house.

Passing the kitchen, she could see Cook pink-cheeked from the heat of the fire and Thomas pouring boiling water into a teapot.

The boy looked up. 'A delivery's come from London, Mrs Holland. The men are bringing it in now.'

The front door was open. Heavy things were being carried in, male voices grumbling and there was Rose rushing down the corridor towards her, her pigtails swinging, her eyes bright. Had the men been flirting with her? It would be simple enough to turn her head.

'For goodness' sake, Rose, what is happening?'

'I weren't sure where to say to put the things Mrs Holland, and it's all for the house ...'

There was a chaotic pile of chairs, boxes, a lamp stand, carpet; household items Mildred recognised from years ago that they had put in storage when they left England.

'They might have been better in the barn while we decided but ...'

Then her heart jumped. Under a piece of furniture, was that one of her travelling trunks? It was over a year since she had seen it. 'Here, help me Rose. Oh, look at this!'

Mildred dragged some packages off the pile and uncovered a battered brown trunk wedged at the bottom. She sank to her knees with a squeal, unable to contain her delight. Unlocking the clasp, she flung open the bulging leather lid. The first thing she noticed was the smell. Slowly, deeply, she inhaled the perfume and now she was back in the busy souk of Rabat.

One afternoon, when the heat had died down a little, their guide had taken William and herself through a warren of turnings to a tiny shop selling scented oils. The owner, insisting they sat on cushioned stools to rest, offered them sweet mint tea in engraved glasses and a bowl of fresh apricots and dates. He brought out a wooden box of phials; uncorked each one to let the heady fragrance infuse into the air, gave her pieces of perfume-soaked cotton to place in her cuff. She had never appreciated before the exquisite sensation of smell. So hard to choose what to buy, they agreed. So several little bottles of perfume were placed in a charming carved box. Now they had come to Huntingfield!

Mildred began to dig in the trunk, wondering what other treasures she would find. Here were items she had craved when she first saw them but had entirely forgotten she owned. Pouches of spice, bunches of brushes, skeins of silk. Swathes of tulle, organza and cotton now tumbled around her in a kaleidoscope of magenta, yellow, pink and vermilion. Some pieces were fringed with gold or tassels or bells, others were sequin-covered or patterned with diamonds and squares. Admiring the fronds of a feathered fan, she cast it aside to grab for a pair of pale green mules. 'My slippers!' she cried, kicking off her shoes and wiggling her toes deliciously in the soft leather.

Now she found her diary, flicked through its pages reading here and there an excerpt of experiences she had almost forgotten. Memories of a dry desert, a bustling market, foreign faces. Sights, smells, tastes, all exhilarating, all unfamiliar. So different from her life in Huntingfield where colours were muted and washed-out, where the sun never shone intensely, where the odours were usually from the farm. How could life change so utterly? How could one person cope with that difference?

A wave of regret pressed on her chest. Mildred realised she was breathing too quickly, shallow breaths that were making her dizzy. She stroked the precious treasures that were strewn around her. Now they are with me, she told herself, perhaps I will feel more at home. I have missed it all very much. She shook her head and gave another sigh.

'Ma'am, anythin' I can do?'

Rose was standing close behind her, frowning.

'Yes, no, I'm fine. Come, I want to show you something. Look, see what I have here.' Mildred held up a little clay pot. Rose looked uncertain. 'It's a lotion, Rose, that the women make from beeswax, almond oil and rose water, yes ... to make the skin soft. Take it,' Mildred said gently, 'it's for you.'

Rose stared suspiciously at the pot that was being offered. She laid it carefully in her palm. Flecks of colour decorated the round lid. With uncertain fingers, she grasped the tiny knob and lifted the lid. She peered inside. Mildred watched the girl take a soft sniff, dip a cautious finger into the pink cream. Even she could detect a whiff of rose and cinnamon as the girl rubbed a blob on to her red knuckle.

'Thank you, Ma'am,' Rose murmured. 'Very kind, I'm sure.'

'I'm glad you like it. Now ... help me with this, will you?'

Mildred was on her feet and had scooped up a swathe of brilliant green silk. But it was more than her arms could manage and the material slithered back to the floor. Smiling at Rose, she said, 'Take each corner and step back over there. Spread it out!'

The women moved towards each end of the hall, arms outstretched, holding the silk. Just then, William came in through the front door. A gust of wind caught the flimsy material. It puffed up into the hallway space, its green brilliance billowing out like a soft giant pea. The women watched as the dome floated and bobbed above them. Sunlight picked out where the weave was loose and tiny shards of light sparkled through. It reminded Mildred of places where bright light was part of every day.

'Look, William, my things are come!' she cried, throwing herself back to her knees and grabbing armfuls of her possessions, she gathered them to herself. But when she looked again at her husband, she saw his face was dark with concern. And then she became aware that tears were falling from her eyes, making damp spots on the materials strewn across her lap.

'Mildred, my dear, stand up.' His voice was toneless. William reached out as though to help her up but she shook him away; why was he trying to prise her away from her things?

'It was wonderful, William, when we were away, it was! Everything we did and saw and now, we are here ...' Mildred began to tremble.

'Rose,' he said gruffly. 'Pack up these things. Put them back in the trunk. Quickly if you will. Thomas, help now and get on with it.'

Why were the servants staring? Mildred buried her head in the gaudy mound and sobbed.

The move to Huntingfield was a shock to her system, said the doctor who William summoned to the Rectory later that evening. It might take her a while to settle down to the countryside after many years of a different sort of life. The doctor prescribed laudanum tablets which would help the still-restless woman to sleep. She needs plenty of rest, he advised, and something to occupy her mind perhaps?

William and Mildred had known each other all their lives. But when William witnessed scenes such as the one this afternoon, he realised how confusing he could find his wife. William and Mildred were first cousins, their fathers being brothers, and they had sung at christenings and cracked nuts at the same Christmas parties all through childhood. It was not until she was 17 that William noticed his curly-haired cousin. She was short, standing only just over five feet three, but what she lacked in height she made up for in a natural energy. Chin held high, she sang with confidence and laughed with obvious enjoyment. He was fascinated by her red-brown curls and green eyes. He knew he wanted to touch her pale skin, to press himself to her round breasts, feelings he'd never had before about a girl – a woman – and he was unsure of what he should do. It took him a full year of dreaming before he finally gathered the courage to speak to her father about the possibility of their marrying at some time in the future.

She was exasperated when she found out. 'William! Why didn't you speak to me directly? It is me you are marrying, not my father!'

'But that is the way it's done, Millie, to ask the father for the girl's hand.'

'I assume that it's not the hand you want to marry, but the woman attached to it!'

This first disagreement was quickly forgotten. But it was obvious to William that Mildred intended to have an equal place in their marriage; she would not defer to her husband as might be expected. She held strong and sometimes different opinions to him; he noticed she was willing to voice them, even in mixed company.

He also knew she could become what he called 'over-wrought'. He remembered an evening early on in their engagement. He was staying with Mildred's family when he was down from Oxford in the holiday. After supper, he and Mildred were reading an article on childbed fever in a periodical William had brought. An Austrian doctor proposed that his medical students, who often went straight from dissecting a dead body to delivering a baby without washing their hands first, carried childbed fever from corpse to woman.

'What nonsense is this? Theirs are healing hands,' William said. 'How could a doctor – a gentleman after all – infect a woman he is caring for?'

'But more women whose babies were delivered by those doctors died than those who were delivered by midwives.'

'Doctors cannot harm their patients! These men are committed and caring.'

'No one is doubting their *intentions*, William. But when the students washed with chlorinated lime, fewer birthing mothers became unwell. Look at the evidence he presents,' said Mildred, stabbing at the page.

'Women have been delivered this way for years.'

'And many die ... as you know!' retorted Mildred.

'Is this not idle speculation, my dear?'

'And you, William Holland, profess an interest in learning?'

'Leave her be,' Mildred's father winked at his future son-in-law as the door slammed. John Holland was a Lincolnshire farmer for whom evenings were best spent eating, drinking and dozing by the fire. 'Millie's spirited, and it doesn't always serve her well,' he said. 'All this talking and arguing, not sure meself if it's good for the women, eh? And suffering, pain, 'tis part of a woman's lot.'

William ordered Thomas to take Mildred's trunk to the attic. It would be stored there until Mildred felt able to unpack it. For the time being, Mildred needed to rest. And she must concentrate on being the Rector's wife; there was plenty she needed to do.

# 4

'I found her kneeling in the attic, Judy, and she were howling like a dog. She wouldn't speak to me. I had to fetch the Rector. Such a commotion.'

Rose was sitting by Judy Scott's bed. Once Sunday lunch at the Rectory was cleared away, Rose was given a half day off to do as she pleased. It gave enough time for her to walk to the village, call in at her sister Mary's cottage to hug her baby niece and promise to return in time for supper, before she was due at Judy's bedside. Judy expected regular snippets of information about the Rectory's inhabitants.

Wife of Ned Scott and mother of five children, all of whom died in the first year of life, Judy had taken to her bed twenty years ago saying she would be dead in three months due to her 'nervous disorganisation'. She did not die. Instead Judy had remained in bed, looked after by the devoted Ned. And she ruled Huntingfield from her bedroom.

Over the years, most families in the village had been involved or associated with something they preferred to forget. Debt, theft, disease, drunkenness, mental unbalance, neighbourly jealousy, incestuous love. All of this Judy knew. All of this Judy remembered. Friends and contacts in the village kept her informed of gossip, news and scandal which she salted away in her excellent memory, ready for use when she deemed it warranted. If slighted or ignored, Judy turned unpleasant. If Judy said a person was odd or strange, few souls in the village were brave enough to question it. A villager could be ostracised on the basis of a single remark. Judy had only to suggest a husband was cheating on his wife, question the paternity of a child, or express doubts about someone's honesty, for life in Huntingfield to become uncomfortable as the scandalous whispering campaign gathered strength.

Most days there was a huddle of women waiting in the Scotts' downstairs room for their turn to ascend to Judy's bedside. And not only women. The Bishop advised Rector Holland he best introduce himself to Judy at the earliest possible opportunity as a way of securing a positive reaction among the villagers.

Judy always saw her visitors individually because, as she assured them, anything told to her was treated in complete confidence. (Everyone knew this was a lie as Judy shared everything she knew when it suited.) If anyone knew what was going on in Huntingfield, it was Judy Scott. And on the basis of what Judy had heard about Mildred Holland, she did not like her.

'Well, she's lived abroad for many years, it's to be expected,' Judy said. 'It's very hot there apparently.'

'Mrs Holland goes out walking every day, even if it's raining. Comes back with the forest stuck on her fine dress, and then I has to pick it off. And then last week, these trunks arrived up from London. Full of strange things, they were, all materials and ornaments, such a gathering of stuff that I've never seen before. She started to cry then too!'

'Did she?'

'I've never seen a rich woman cry,' Rose stated.

'I think you'll find they have tears very much like our own,' Judy sniped.

'We had to put her trunks away up in the attic where she can't see them. And the doctor was called, all the way from Laxfield, and he give her something to settle her. She went to sleep after. The Rector looked right worried.'

'She is a strange woman, that Mrs Holland, from what I hear,' said Judy, fixing the bows on her bonnet under her chin. She was always careful to be well turned out for her visitors and though Rose was only a servant girl, Judy had her reputation to maintain.

'Ned, I say Ned, bring me my shawl, thank you dear!' Her voice was polite enough but her tone suggested a quick response was required. Within a moment her husband appeared in the room.

'It's been washed and aired, my dear. Now you wrap up.' And tucking the shawl tenderly around Judy's shoulders, he shuffled off back down the stairs.

Ned had looked after Judy patiently; ran the household, grew the vegetables and took odd jobs for cash when work came along. His wife, by comparison, had lain in bed orchestrating life from under the blankets. Their different ways of living may not have had a bearing on the way they aged, but he was bent and bowed while she had an unlined face.

'Pass me the mirror, girl.'

'She's kind to me, mind,' said Rose, handing Judy a mirror and watching as she tucked away a stray piece of hair. 'She's given me things, these shoes, look Judy! And for Mary's baby, some lovely cloth. I gave it to Mary and she were pleased. And Mrs Holland treated the rash on me arm that was dreadful sore.'

'Treated you, did she? Is she a doctor, then?' asked Judy

sarcastically. 'And why would a lady like her give you, a servant girl, presents if you don't mind? I don't like it, not at all.'

It went through Rose's mind that she was being disloyal to Mildred, telling Judy about her tears and upsets. Since the first day she and William had arrived at the Rectory, Mildred had been kind to Rose. Very different from the previous Rector's wife. Mrs Uthoff used sharp words and commands, even slapped her hand once when she'd burnt the toast. The Uthoffs had not put up Rose's wage for over ten years. As for gratitude, Rose had never been given a present before. Rose shifted uncomfortably and said: 'She is a friendly lady, and kind in her way. And Mr Holland is a gentleman.'

'But why is she friendly?' insisted Judy, sitting up in bed as straight as she could. 'Here, fix me my pillows, Rose. It don't make sense, girl, not to me. There's something strange in that woman. Why don't they have no children?'

Sometimes in the morning when William left on parish business, Mildred would wander around the bedroom wondering how to make the hours pass. During the day, it is so quiet. I would use the words deadly, she whispered, but I would find that terrifying.

Living in Huntingfield was like living under snow, she decided. Not just because it was cold but because all the sounds were muffled and movements were laborious. She sat at the bedroom window, looking out over the dark heads of her friends, the yew trees, to the open country that stretched out to the horizon. It was almost still, the smoke from a cottage chimney in the distance the only sign of human life. The sky dominated, so vast that she must turn her head, left to right, as far as it would go to see where the horizon began and where it ended. A wood pigeon flew by; its strangulated call was startling, and her heart jumped.

Once a week she took a woodland path Rose called 'The Causeway' into Huntingfield village. There was a post office, a tailor, an inn, a cobbler and a blacksmith. Mildred loved to watch men at work; the cobbler crouched over his tools, stretching and sewing, cutting and polishing leather. The smell reminded her of workshops she had visited in Rabat. Or she would stand by the blacksmith's forge, twitching as he smacked the hammer down on the metal and the bellow-breath of the furnace made red sparks fly and crackle.

Sometimes a woman had set up a stall to sell the glut of her garden's fruit and vegetables. Mildred knew the few coins she handed over might be the only money that household had for some time. And there was always the chance of a few minutes of talk with one of the villagers, those who did not avoid her, at least. The weather, the health of the children, it would become easier as she got to know the people, she reassured herself. Sometimes she wondered if this would ever be true.

Each morning Thomas brought news from the village, reports of illnesses or accidents, and she and William would then discuss what best could be done to help. If William was too busy or the case was of a delicate nature, it would be up to Mildred to call on the family. Visiting parish families was what a rector's wife should do and Mildred was inclined to undertake her responsibilities. But she had to admit to herself or to God – she wasn't sure which – that she didn't enjoy the work. When the day ahead was one of parish visits, she felt weary and despondent and only after a several strong cups of tea did the feelings subside. The villagers did not like her. It was as simple as that.

Mildred always considered carefully what she should take with her. Medicines and bandages, bread or a pie, butter, matches, salt? Money was appreciated, she knew that, although one could never be sure that the cash was going to be spent on the doctor's bill rather than at the tavern.

The first knock on a family's door needed courage: she was never sure what she might find or what the response might be. Once she'd called on a family whose children were reported to have measles. In a dark cottage, she found two children, covered with spots and bright-eyed with fever, stretched out on a stinking bed. Groans came from the back room. There was a woman, presumably their mother, almost delirious with fever, a line of sores running down her trunk, and whispering for her husband. Had he absconded to the tavern?

She wrote to her sister:

*I spent the rest of the day applying calamine lotion to the children's blisters and cider vinegar to the mother's shingles. Of course, I wanted to apply a pan to the head of that dreadful father when he stumbled in the door drunk later that evening. Elizabeth, what kind of a man could leave his family in such a state?*

On another occasion when they were told that Mrs Tippett had a swollen abdomen not thought to be a pregnancy, Mildred called at the cottage with basket of food and money. A man opened the door, glared at her, took the goods without a word and slammed the door. She was devastated when Thomas told her a few days later that the woman had died of a burst appendix. Why would the family not accept her help?

In a sunny spot in the garden, Mildred started to sketch; a quick drawing of the salesman's beaming face when he'd sold Rose his potion. She would send the doodle to Elizabeth; her sister always loved her drawings which made her laugh. How did Elizabeth stay so cheerful? Never having married, she remained in the family home caring for their elderly parents. Each day must be very like every other day for Elizabeth, too. How could one sister cope so well while the other wriggled like a worm on a hook?

Mildred flicked through her drawing book. A sketch of a gargoyle, a statue, a fountain, a busy market, scenes which she and William had watched together. Reaching for her hat, the sun hot on her nose reminded her of happy travelling days, and she was happy to remember them. Languages she did not understand, facial features she did not recognise, landscapes that sometimes terrified her with their foreignness. The sensation of uncertainty, how she loved that! No prescribed way to how she might feel or react; simply experience.

Two men were working on the roof of the church. A scaffolding of wooden poles clung like a lizard to the building and from this makeshift platform, one handed a tile or tool to the other. She couldn't hear what they said but they were laughing and joking. One man wiped his head with a handkerchief; it flashed white against the blue sky.

'What can you see from up there?' she called. They hadn't seen her among the gravestones. Two quizzical faces peered down from the scaffolding.

'Good day, Mrs Holland.' They nodded but it was awkward with their heads hanging downwards.

'How far can you see? Can you see the coast?'

She stood near the ladder which leaned against a scaffolding post. A thought flashed through her head: she wanted to climb up it. She shook her head; she mustn't, the men would think it very strange.

'Just mending the roof, Mrs Holland,' called down one of the men. 'We can see Bramfield where the hay's being cut in one of the fields and ...'

With a wave of her hand, she went into the church. The walls had been repaired and whitewashed. A table was strewn with tools and a window had been mended. There was a broom propped up against the wall; the place had been swept clean of leaves and dirt. Everywhere she looked there was evidence of people taking action, being in the world, taking part. They were free to act. Was it what they themselves would have chosen? Perhaps for others her life appeared privileged, full of choice and replete with freedom. It was not the case. She felt herself to be only a bystander in her own life; destined never to be an active principal, fated only to watch others.

'I won't have supper tonight, Rose, I've no appetite. Just one lamp.' Mildred collapsed in a chair as though exhausted by labour.

Rose pulled the parlour curtains shut, fed the fire and left the room. Her footsteps died away. The house was still. Bleak thoughts crept in as they often did when the dark edges of the room, where fire and lamplight failed to penetrate, mirrored those parts of her mind where memories lay buried until shaken awake by stillness. Humiliating memories: examinations and appointments in various European centres of excellence when medical men made intrusive enquiries about the couple's intimate relations; her body poked and probed with cold metal instruments; the fruitless search for the answer to the question posed every time the monthly mark of blood confirmed that no baby grew in her womb. And here, despite their prayers, still no baby came.

# 5

'Good morning, Mrs Holland.' Harry Browne, the postmaster, waved an impatient hand at the line of villagers, indicating they should stand aside as Mildred entered his shop.

'Please, Mr Browne, please, do carry on. I will wait until you have finished.'

At the back of the shop, the shelves of tinned and dry goods held little interest but she could eavesdrop on the conversation at the counter. The tinkle of coins and murmured voices suggested Poor Law relief money was being handed over. Mildred knew it caused a rift in the village, this monetary handout given to some when so many others struggled to make ends meet. It is unfair, they argued, that some should work while others did not. Mildred had stepped over people starving in the streets of London, Paris and Rome. Poverty was horrible and degrading, and she did not want to see it in her village. There needed to be relief for families who struggled to survive.

In William's view the village should look after its own. Tackling poverty needed practical solutions. So he offered employment whenever possible and tried to persuade others, the farmers and landowners, that morally they were obliged to do the same. William purchased several cottages in the village which he rented at low rates to poorer families so they could avoid the Union House.

Mildred knew that local pockets would never be deep enough to protect the village from the winds of change that threatened it. The Industrial Revolution might roar in distant parts of the country but its heat was felt in Huntingfield. Two families had recently left for the promise of employment in a factory town in the Midlands. And who could blame them when traditional jobs were becoming obsolete? Steam power not only drove the new factories but also the threshing machines and grain mills, reducing the need for workers. Spinning and weaving which used to give women the chance to earn a bit of extra cash was being done by machines.

Everyone knew the old ways were changing fast. Common land, places where people had been able to gather fuel, graze a pig or keep a few hens, was now fenced in. Some who had once owned a little parcel of land were tempted by the lure of quick cash to sell to a local farmer, but later regretted it. And the new Game Laws were fearsome. Taking a pheasant or hare, tolerated in the past if it was understood it was done to ease hunger, was now called 'poaching'. It was a crime for which a labourer could be transported to Australia.

Huntingfield was luckier than some villages. Heveningham Hall provided employment for many who lived in its shadow; full-time work in the house or casual work when the hunting parties were lavish. The making and repairing of roads had made it easier to travel around; it also meant that the pool of people from which servants could be drawn was larger than before. If an employer did not like the service offered by one person, there were plenty of others who were willing to supply it.

Mildred peered over the shelf. It was hard to tell because her shawl was pulled across her face but wasn't that woman Jane Thomas? Mildred had heard that her husband, Andrew, had lost his job a few weeks ago. He had been late for work one morning and the farm manager had sacked him on the spot. Perhaps hung-over, Andrew had lashed out. The manager's whistle summoned the farm dogs and Andrew was savagely attacked. It was left to his wife Jane and neighbours to nurse the injured man back to recovery, and to Jane to fend for their four children. Mildred had visited the Thomases' cottage soon after the incident. When she knocked, Jane's drawn face peered around the door.

'What d'ya want?' She glared at Mildred suspiciously, her red-rimmed eyes narrowed. From inside the cottage, she could hear children crying, then a growling complaint followed by a slap and a wail.

'I've brought some food, and some money, too. We were sorry to hear about Andrew's accident.'

A pale arm slid out from behind the door and took the offered basket. 'Many thanks, Mrs Holland,' said Jane, and the door began to scrape shut.

'Jane. I wonder … are you good with a needle? I have some darning that needs doing and I am not handy myself.'

Jane had agreed to take the work. She returned to the Rectory a few days later, wrapped up against the wind, the mending tied in a clean, white handkerchief.

'Goodness Jane, you have been quick, and it's beautifully done! Thank you.' The woman would not meet Mildred's eyes. She looked exhausted. 'Here, let me fetch your pay. I don't have the exact money but …' Mildred handed over a few extra coins. 'There's change owed, Mrs Holland,' said Jane stiffly. 'I don't have it with me at the moment but I'll send one of the girls up tomorrow.'

'No, next time will be fine, Jane, there will be more darning. If you're willing?'

That was a few weeks ago. No doubt the money had helped but it was not enough; Jane was queuing for assistance.

The doorbell jingled. A slight dark-haired woman entered the shop. She was holding the hand of a small girl who looked just like her. It was Ann, the young wife of a local lawyer, Richard Owen. Mildred and Ann had met at the garden fete held at Heveningham Hall a few weeks earlier. Richard was advising William on buying property in the village.

'Hallo Mildred. Good day to you,' Ann had a deep voice, low for a woman. Mildred remembered the woman's childish delight when she won the tombola, slipping the little figurine she'd won into her pocket with a giggle.

'This is our elder daughter, Sarah. Say good day to Mrs Holland.'

The little girl shook Mildred's hand solemnly and stood sucking her finger.

'Hallo, Sarah. It is very nice to meet you. What beautiful brown eyes you have. I saw you at the fair on the swings with your sister.' Mildred knelt down.

'Have you come to post a letter?'

She told Sarah about some newborn puppies she'd seen at one of the village cottages, then bought the girl a bag of sweets to share with her sisters. The women chatted for a few minutes. 'That is a beautiful scarf Mildred. Such wonderful colours,' said Ann.

'Yes, isn't it? I'm not sure if William mentioned it to your husband, but William and I travelled across the Continent for many years before we took up the living in Huntingfield. I bought this in Egypt from a small workshop outside Alexandria.'

'Egypt? You've travelled on the Continent? How exotic, Mrs

Holland, how fascinating! I have never left this country. Oh, you must tell me more. Would you be willing to call on us for tea? You'd be most welcome. We live just outside the village, down a track near the Hall, not far from you.' Ann was insistent. 'You can meet my other daughter, Grace, and we can sit in the garden, and you can tell me about your travels. Say you will, do!'

As she started back for the Rectory, Mildred found herself humming. In her pocket, her fingers touched the piece of sticky sugar she had saved from Sarah's bag of sweets. Picking off a piece of lint, she popped it in her mouth, licked the sweetness from her fingertips.

She decided against taking her usual path home and instead followed a trail which meandered through a copse of young silver birch trees, elegant as whips. Her skirts rustled the dry grass, bent by some passing animal perhaps. Beyond some alder bushes hung with butter-yellow catkins, a patch of wood sorrel grew on a mossy log. She touched the cup-shaped flowers, ran her fingers along the milky-white petals laced by fine mauve veins. The warm ground smelt earthy. A black beetle scuttled over the toe of her boot.

Squatting among the plants, for the first time in ages she felt content. If she could make a new friend, someone with her interests, perhaps. Gathering cowslips and buttercups into an untidy bunch, she pushed on through undergrowth and found herself at the back of the Rectory. Trees grew up to the garden wall, brambles scrambled over the brick, matted and persistent. Sometimes when she looked out from the Rectory, it seemed to her that Nature threatened to overwhelm them, as though the trees would march through the wall and smother them. Today she felt only the peace of the deep green wood.

~

Mildred took special care as she dressed that day. Standing at the mirror, she carefully set a grey bonnet on her head, tucking under her curls, and pinned the pearl brooch which William bought her in Rome on to a pretty lace collar. Why am I so pleased? she asked her reflection. Going to tea with another woman hardly ranked as an exciting event. But there was something about Ann Owen which was intriguing. She said less than she felt. Ann was unlike the other women in the area; not a gossip who nursed tedious concerns or one to voice petty criticisms of others.

A present – Mildred would bring Ann a present! But what? An idea dawned on her, and Mildred reached under the bed to drag out a large box. Flicking open the catch, she rifled through layers of material; velvet, lace, satin, silk, until finally she stopped at a flash of bright green. She tugged out a length of gauze which, caught on a draught, floated around Mildred's face. Its cool smooth surface caressed her face, a hint of perfume wafted by. With a piece of gold ribbon, she made it into a pretty bundle.

'You're off to tea with Mrs Owen? When will you be back?' said William.

'I'm only there for tea. I might miss prayers, I do hope you won't mind that tonight, dear?'

'No, of course, not. Have a good time then Millie. My regards to Ann and, if you see Richard, please send him my best also.'

William watched his wife step up into the trap and blew her a kiss. He waved as she was driven down the long driveway and out of the gate into the lane, and wandered back to his study.

He was exasperated. When they lay together in bed, he would stroke her arms and face and he would be tempted to ask her if she was happy in Huntingfield. But in truth he did not want her answer and so the question was not posed. For if she were to acknowledge her unhappiness, William would have to do something about it.

Since becoming the Rector, William's life had broadened. There were sermons to write, services to take, plans for the new school, plenty to fulfil him. By contrast, beyond running the house and visiting the sick, there was little to engage Mildred. The few people she met in the locality she claimed were parochial and prone to gossip, and she refused subsequent invitations to tea at Heveningham Hall saying she found Lady Huntingfield and her cronies dull. Perhaps Ann Owen would become a friend? He should feel happy for Mildred, not irritated!

He also knew why the villagers found his wife unsettling but this he would not be able to explain to her. For it went to the heart of the kind of person that Mildred was. She was unconventional, walking to the village rather than taking the carriage, for example, and going hatless. He suspected the villagers found her unpredictable. Sometimes she sympathised with people in distress and made great efforts to understand their difficulties, but at other times, she appeared distracted and disinterested. People in the village had expectations of their parish Rector and his wife; to act always in the same grand and haughty way, and to dispense their generosity with dependable condescension.

In William's mind, there was no question or debate about the natural order. He was the Rector and his place in life was to bring spiritual comfort to his flock. He expected – and received – the villagers' respect and their gratitude. If he couldn't provide all the answers, he could point to the mysterious ways of the Lord as something which his humble servants, like himself, must accept without question. William exuded certainty, and in some indefinable way, that made things simpler for those around him. William was the Rector and the villagers, whether they were believers or thought it was all a load of poppycock, accepted him. People knew where they were with William. With Mildred, they could never be sure.

William adored Mildred and lived with the comfortable illusion that he would do anything to help her. But this was not true. Deep down – and this was something he could not admit to himself – his commitment to her rubbed sharp against what he felt was right and proper. She *ought* to be happy. He was, after all! They had spent eight years on the Continent, preparing for their life in Huntingfield – and now it had begun. He must continue to pray for her.

The trap swung through the grand entrance of Heveningham Hall and halfway up the sweeping drive took a turn up a rutted track. Skirting a row of trees, the trap pulled up at a low brick house. Squawking geese startled the horse. There was Ann. She clapped her hands to shoo the honking birds away and hurried over to Mildred. 'Sorry about that welcome. Please, come in!' she called. 'It is good to see you here, at last.'

The house was modest, smaller than the Rectory, but comfortable enough. The women went down the hall, stepping over a bed of rags where a mother cat lay nursing a litter of kittens, past the nursery where two girls were quarrelling at a piano and beyond the kitchen where the clatter of cutlery and squalls of fishy steam suggested high tea was being prepared. They stepped out of the back door into the garden.

'Peace!' Ann laughed. 'Come into the garden house. It looks like it might rain. When does William expect you back?'

It was cold in the weak sunshine but the little garden house grew warm as the women talked. Ann explained she had two children: Sarah whom Mildred had met at the shop was eight years old and Grace who was five.

'And another on the way,' Ann said ruefully.

'Congratulations, that is a great blessing.'

'It is, of course. You and the Reverend have no children?'

'No. We pray and hope that it will happen one day.' Mildred hoped her tone indicated that this particular conversation should end. 'So tell me, Ann. Where is your family from?'

Both women had been born into large extended families; parents, siblings, aunts, uncles and cousins who had all lived in close proximity to each other. There had always been someone to talk to or to visit. Regular family events and celebrations, feuds and fights! But in Suffolk, with their husbands busy with work, they could go days without seeing another person apart from the servants.

'It's blissful!' said Ann. 'After all those years of chaos, to be here, away from prying eyes and gossip, to do what I wish. Of course I miss my family and I go to visit with the children from time to time, but that's enough for me. To be away from sitting rooms and stilted talk, free to do what I want, I prefer it. I go into Huntingfield as little as possible. I send Hannah, our girl, if I can, and if it means I must do the cooking, so be it. I find village people suspicious.'

Mildred nodded. 'They may call it respect but I feel they treat me with disdain. I'm a stranger in these parts ... perhaps it's not surprising. I make them feel uncomfortable, I think; I am not sure why.' She sighed. 'I didn't know better when I gave the housemaid a pot of cream I'd bought in Constantinople. Her mother had a fit. She tried to throw it on to the fire, thought it was jinxed!'

'I'm happy here with my children and my creatures. See over there.' Ann pointed to a large wired cage where brightly-coloured birds perched and flew about. 'Canaries. Exquisite things, don't you think? And with the sweetest song. I love to watch them. More enchanting than our grumpy geese though not so good at guarding us!'

A sudden shower of hail drumming on the glass roof made Mildred jump.

'Look Ann, the girls. They're worried about you.' Over at the house, Sarah and Grace had their faces pressed to the window.

The women waved, laughing.

'I must go once this shower has passed. But before I do ... look, I've brought this for you.' Mildred handed Ann the green parcel. 'I'd like you to have this.'

Even in the gloom of the rainy afternoon, the iridescent green and gold threads of the scarf glimmered. Ann looked stunned. 'Are you sure Mildred? For me?'

Mildred nodded; she could not regret giving this precious object away to someone who would appreciate it so much. She watched Ann stroke the silk against her cheek.

'I saw it being made by a woman in a Marrakesh souk. Squatting on a carpet, she was spinning the threads of silk as if playing an enchanted instrument.'

Pleasure spread across Ann's face as she draped the material around her neck. 'It's beautiful, thank you.'

It was refreshing to meet a woman with an original mind, Mildred thought, on the way back to Huntingfield. I am not usually so open with a person I have barely met, but I feel I can trust her; she understands what I say and she doesn't judge me. One day I will tell her everything.

# 6

1850 SPRING

'She is just so rude, William. It's too much!'

Mildred stood by the table, biting her lip. She pulled off her hat and with a gesture of anger that he rarely saw, flung it across the room.

'My dear, sit down. What's happened? Who has upset you? I thought you had gone to see Judy Scott?' William walked towards her but she gestured him away.

'She's so cold, so unkind, with her cutting remarks, poking me with words. Not you, William, she speaks with the highest regard about *you*!' Mildred sat down with a thump on the chair that William had drawn up to the fire. She looked at him, her eyes bright with anger. 'It's me. All the villagers hate me. I shouldn't let it upset me, I know. But it does. It's too bad.'

It had been a beautiful March morning, warm for the time of year and very dry. She had walked quickly through the woods into the village, the scent of wild garlic on her palm as she waved it across their white frilly heads. The fat buds in the hedgerows added to the air of expectancy; everything seemed to long for spring. She was cheerful.

A stone path led up to the cottage door. The blue paint was

peeling but the knocker had recently been polished and shone in the sunlight. By the door, little clumps of primroses, daffodils and crocuses grew in the cracked soil. The rest of the garden had been neatly dug in rows, waiting for the rain when planting could start. There was not a weed to be seen.

'Good morning, Mr Scott. It's Mrs Holland.' The door opened and Ned Scott's face, haggard and lined, looming out of the dark like a pale phantom. He strained sideways to see her face, unable to lift his head directly upwards because of his humped back. He indicated she should enter. It was hard to see where to place her foot in the gloomy room. She found herself chattering as though her words might light up the interior.

'And how is Judy today? Do tell her I've come to call. Thank you, Mr Scott. If you wouldn't mind, thank you.'

'Come in.' He finally spoke. 'I'll tell her you are here.'

Ned shuffled over to close the front door and then she heard him slowly climb the stairs, each step seeming to take an eternity. Mildred perched on a wooden bench and looked around.

The curtains were closed. A single chair by the fire, a cupboard with a few of pieces of china and a small table. It was spotless, like Ned. She'd noticed his nails, very clean and white, and his carefully patched shirt and trousers. Only the thatch of eyebrow hair showed he was not in total control.

A few minutes later Ned returned. 'You can go up if you please, Mrs Holland,' he nodded.

Judy was tucked up in bed, a bonnet neatly tied under her chin. Mildred saw an open Bible lying on the bedclothes. Judy was keen on the Bible. That was one of the reasons William Mildred to visit.

'She's an intelligent woman,' he had said, 'well versed in the Bible and keen to discuss the Scriptures. The previous Rector spoke of her highly. Always grateful to converse with persons of a superior education, I understand.'

'Hallo Judy. How are you today?' Mildred stood by the door.

Judy regarded her from the bed. 'Ah, Mrs Holland, do sit down. How kind of you to visit. How is the dear Rector?'

'Very well, thank you.'

'Such a talented man. We are indeed blessed that he is here to live and to work among us. He is kind enough to visit from time to time, a visit I always enjoy for he is so clever, so well educated.'

Mildred sensed the comment was barbed.

Judy continued: 'The Rector was kind enough to mention that he is building a new school for the village. It will be up near the Rectory, I understand, and the children will receive more religious education than they do at present. Well, that is a good thing for they are sometimes a little unruly, would you not agree?'

Walking through the village one day, Mildred had almost been knocked over by a swarm of children running from one of the cottages. A woman appeared in the door, shouting after them as they charged along the main street. 'And you come back tomorrow mind or I'll give you a hiding you won't forget!'

She was surprised to learn that this was the 'School Mistress' Miss Bobby, who had run a 'dame' school in the village for over twenty years. The truth was that the school had a poor reputation; many pupils left at the age of ten, unable to read or write. They also had a familiarity with Miss Bobby's hand which suggested rough treatment.

'That is so,' Mildred agreed. 'I have found the children very noisy in the street.'

Judy's reaction was swift. 'I take it you are not criticising the great service that Miss Bobby has provided to the children of Huntingfield all these years, Mrs Holland?'

'No, not all,' Mildred said hastily. 'The village will always be grateful to Miss Bobby for all that she has done. But children can be a handful, and now that she has decided to retire, William is happy to provide a fresh start.'

Indeed, William had talked of little else but the school for some months now, Mildred reflected ruefully. In her prayers, she sometimes asked God if he could find William another subject to talk about soon.

'William will make sure the school has high standards,' said Mildred. 'With a more rigorous curriculum: religious studies, arithmetic and so on.'

Judy nodded. 'This is very good news. Thank the Lord, the eternal God, and Creator of the earth. He never gets weary or tired; His wisdom cannot be measured. Isaiah 40.' She sat up straighter, patting the Bible with satisfaction. 'I understand there is also to be a Sunday school.' She sat forward and peered at Mildred. 'Perhaps you will lead the school yourself, Mrs Holland? One learns so much oneself when instructing others, don't you think, Mrs Holland?'

The tone was accusatory but Judy's face was all innocence. 'Children are so easily influenced. Of course it is important to set the best example,' Mildred murmured.

Judy swivelled her head to look pointedly at Mildred. 'One must always do and behave in the *right* way. Very important, don't you agree?'

Mildred said: 'We will interview a number of schoolmasters and their wives. Perhaps one of those women will run the school.'

'With the Rector away a great deal, *you* must have a good deal of time on your hands?'

Mildred winced inwardly. How could Judy know how little interest she had in teaching Sunday school?

Mildred stood up. She felt unsettled by this prying woman.

As brightly as she could muster she said, 'I will visit again soon if I may? The Rector sends his regards and says he will come later this week to give you Communion. I hope we may see Ned at service this Sunday? Good day to you.'

Mildred left the room, certain she could feel Judy's steely eyes boring into her back. She cannot see around corners, Mildred told herself stepping gingerly down the steep stairs. It just feels like she can.

# 7

---

1853 SPRING

Five letters in one day! All but one was addressed to William.

'We've received three applications for the schoolmaster's position at the new village school, Millie. That is very good news indeed.' William was pleased. 'And a letter from Sydney Pegler, my old friend from Oxford.'

She handed him a cup of tea.

'Help me consider the applications, will you Millie? I need your good sense to help me judge the suitability of these candidates.'

'Of course, I'll save Elizabeth's letter until later. There's no great rush.'

'Here is one from Mr Clark and his wife. They sound an interesting couple with a wealth of experience.'

He passed her their letter and accepted a slice of cake.

'It seems most of the time they have been working for a school in a small town and more recently for another in Bristol city. Crumb on your lip, my dear. How would they cope in a little place like this, do you think?'

'You may be right. Here's one from a Miss Cooper. A young

woman born and raised in Yorkshire so she'd be accustomed to the peace of Huntingfield,' said William flicking his eyes over her application. 'Rather young, only in her early twenties. Would she miss her family very much, I wonder?'

'That's why the job might suit a couple like the Goulds. Look at these people.' She passed across a letter. 'They've worked in a small school for over five years. Reading between the lines, they ended up running the school when the owner fell ill.'

'He feels music is important for young pupils and she is a pianist. Marvellous!' William read on. 'And they want to move to Suffolk because she has family connections in the area.' He peered over his glasses at her, grinning. 'The Goulds sound most suitable.'

Mildred handed William another cup of tea.

'It's exciting to think we can finally make an appointment for next term,' said William. 'The building will be finished at last and we'll be ready for the pupils. I mention it at every Sunday service and when I go into the village. But I do sense some reluctance.'

'Is it to do with where the school is? A mile out of the village. Perhaps parents don't want to be so far from their children.'

'Perhaps they're worried I'll call in at the school during the day and notice if their child is absent. I know parents sometimes keep the children at home to help with farm work. Did I tell you? I wrote to the Bishop and told him I plan to offer a small stipend for every child who attends school for the full day. He thinks it's a marvellous idea. I suspect that will increase numbers.'

'I suspect it will.' She nodded. 'You are a very good man, Rector Holland. Kind and generous.'

William beamed. 'Millie dear, Sydney has a son, James, who is taking the Oxford entrance examination in October. He wants me to give the boy some extra tuition as preparation: Latin, maths, philosophy. He hopes he could stay here for a month so I can tutor him. Will that suit?'

What possible reason could she give for saying no?

Rose and Thomas managed the house with only a little guidance and if Mildred noticed a dust ball in the corridor, she tended to look the other way. Cook's meals were enjoyable and her baking delicious. William certainly found it so; his trousers needed letting out around the waist. Thank goodness Jane was handy with the needle and keen to have the work. Mildred visited needy families in the village and there was the occasional social event which she generally avoided. Of course, visits with Ann and the girls were always welcome; Ann was becoming a firm friend. But the prospect of a house guest would make a change.

'That will be fine, dear,' she said. 'I look forward to meeting your young Mr James Pegler. I'll speak to Rose and she can get a room ready. Where will you do the teaching?'

William left to visit one of parish farms. Mildred drifted upstairs to their bedroom. Rose had made the bed and emptied the chamber pot but there was her dressing table to arrange. The silver hairbrush given her as a wedding present needed polishing. On its tarnished back, the initials M and W were intertwined. She sat at the dressing table and slowly pulled out the pins holding her hair. It fell on to her shoulders, still thick even if the red had dulled. An obstinate strand of white hair sprang out fiercely at the temple and she tugged it out. It floated out of the window; she followed its flight as it wafted down into the garden.

A cart went up the lane; perhaps the last load of materials for the school house. Banging and sawing, she liked the noise; it meant things were happening. She studied her face in the mirror. Freckles were not fashionable but there they were, sprinkled across her nose and cheeks like brown sugar. As soon as the sun came out, more came to greet it. She must wear a hat this summer, she thought, although she hated to keep off the sun. It reminded her of hot Italian afternoons when she and William escaped the blaring white light of the streets for the cool of their bedroom and the warmth of their passion.

It will be good to have a young man to stay here, she told herself, even if William has to push the poor boy through exams. She opened her letter.


*Dear Millie,*

*Mother has recovered from her cold and Father takes her out each day for a walk. It does them both good and I am sure that it stimulates her appetite. They are well wrapped against the cold. As she is not steady on her feet, the doctor came yesterday and has provided a strong stick. He is pleased with her progress. So all is now returning to its usual routine.*

*However, my dear sister, I remain concerned about you. I remember our conversations by the fire in the months before you married. You knew then that life in the village was going to be quiet. You were happy to accept it then, so remember our conversations and be strong, my darling sister! I know that with God's good grace, you can remain a cheery and good wife to William, despite the disappointments you suffer. Here is a card you sent me from Constantinople which I have treasured for the last five years. I return it to you in the hope that it may grant your wish for a child.*

*Your loving sister, Elizabeth.*

. . .

It was a drawing of St Margaret of Antioch, the patron saint of women. Margaret had been brave, so Mildred must be too! One day soon her prayers would be answered. She would be pregnant and have the children that both she and William dreamed of raising here in Huntingfield. Mildred kissed the card, propped it up against a bottle of perfume, and then went to talk to Cook about meals for their guest.

'We live a quiet life in Huntingfield. I hope you won't find us too dull.'

Mildred put another piece of cake on James Pegler's plate. The splatters of mud across his riding habit showed how unsettled the weather had been since he'd ridden from the family home in Essex three days ago. The poor boy was clearly starving. Mildred called for more tea and poked at the fire; she felt pleased.

'William will be back later for prayers and then we'll have a short service followed by supper. Will that suit you? And give your wet clothes to Rose when you change.'

The boy ate and drank with a degree of concentration only seen in the young. Thank goodness he wasn't like his father, whose air of self-importance was ridiculed by the pince-nez that gripped his nose so tightly that he squinted. James was poised, even over-confident for an eighteen-year-old. But there was something about him, an assumption of his place in the world which she found amusing. He seemed to know what he wanted and how he might get it, but in such a charming way that you could not possibly mind.

'Thank you for allowing me to stay here,' he said politely. He wiped his mouth on a napkin and sat back comfortably, crossing one muddy riding boot on his knee. 'I sit the Oxford entrance exams in just over a month. My father is concerned that I won't pass. Not warranted in my opinion, I will do well. He hopes that studying with Mr Holland will increase my chances.'

'You hope to go up to Oxford? What plans after that? I understand your father wants you to be ordained.'

'He does. And it is important that I get a place at Oxford to pursue his ... that ... plan.'

His blue eyes, set slightly far apart, gave a clear message. This boy did not want to do what his father expected of him. She wondered how Sydney, so confident of his views, so vehement with his opinions, would deal with a recalcitrant son, especially one as articulate as this boy. James concentrated on the next bite of Cook's fruit cake. Dark curly hair tumbled over a pale complexion, long delicate fingers picked at the crumbs; a relaxed folding of his frame as he reached for a sandwich, pausing only to look up for her nod of approval that he should do so.

She decided not to enquire further. 'There's building work going on here, did you see it? We're having a school built for the children of the village. The Bishop of Norwich is encouraging his clergy to improve educational standards in the villages and William is following that request.'

'What do the villagers think?'

'A mixed reaction, I would say,' she smiled, handing him another cup of tea. 'They don't like change, you know.'

'And you, Mrs Holland, how do you occupy yourself living here, as you say, in this quiet place?'

The question made her start. It was as though he had reached out and touched her, as though he sensed her discontent. Did she hesitate for a moment?

'Life may be quiet but we are busy. With the parish, the household, we visit families in need, when there is sickness or trouble ...'

'Yes, of course, I appreciate there are the duties that a rector and his wife must fulfil and that would, of course, keep one occupied.' He paused. 'It was more a question to you, Mrs Holland. I am curious about what *you* do here, for yourself?'

Thinking about the conversation later as she changed for supper, she was not sure why he asked this question. He could not possibly be interested in her reply. Perhaps it was a question he was asking of himself; he wanted to understand how people managed to live lives that were not of their choosing. She sensed that he resisted the thought that he might have to comply with a life he did not want.

Despite this, she had found herself telling James about her interest in drawing and painting; how she would soon set up a small studio at the Rectory so she could carry on with this work. She surprised herself with her own conviction. She had not articulated these thoughts even to herself; it had never felt so clear to her that this was what she wanted as it did when she described it to James. It was as though a part of her which had been asleep was awake, alert. As she voiced her plans, they began to feel real and achievable. It is odd, she reflected later, to realise what it is you want to do by telling it to someone else.

'Apparently there was blood shooting *everywhere*.' Rose stood by Judy's bed, her eyes wide with horror. 'Poor John, the doctor had to take off the leg, right there in the stable.'

'I could hear the yelling.' There was disgust in Judy's voice. 'As that leg came off, he was screaming. Sally always says her husband John is a brave man but from what I heard, he made a terrible fuss.'

'Judy! I 'spect it hurt something terrible, with only the brandy the Rector sent over helping to ease his pain.'

'At least he didn't lose his life. He should be grateful for that,' quipped Judy unkindly. 'If Owen Walton had not wrapped that leg in sacking, John Hammant would have bled to death. That's what the doctor told Ned.' Judy wiggled like a hen getting comfortable on a nest of eggs. 'I know because I sent Ned off to have a word as the doctor was leaving the cottage.'

Rose winced: Judy could be cruel. Sometimes she only seemed interested in intrigue and other people's misfortunes, sniffing out gossip to cause trouble. Rose wondered if she really had to come every Sunday to report to the old woman. It's what she'd done ever since starting work at the Rectory but ...

Rose Goody had three hopes for her life. After saying her prayers, she would lie in her narrow bed and think through each one. To marry and have children like her sister Mary (that new house guest, James Pegler, would suit her well – but no, even dreams had to be realistic), to visit the Tower of London where the murderers were hung to death, and to own a piece of amber jewellery from the shop in Southwold. But sometimes Rose thought she would risk it all to have one piece of information that Judy did *not* know, and to drop that information into Judy's ear when she, Rose, was good and ready.

Judy warned: 'Sally has a lot on her hands now. Three girls to feed and a useless husband too. She'll have to go on outdoor relief.' The woman was almost gloating. 'If Sally don't watch it, it's the workhouse for that family.'

It became obvious over the next few weeks that James had little appetite for study. He did everything he could to distract William from the Latin or maths lesson he was being given. He was much more interested in talking about politics, science, William's plans for the school, local farming practices, chatting with Rose – anything rather than his work. Questions of theology or the reality of life as a rector he did not raise and, while James dutifully attended morning and evening prayers, William was not convinced he had the faith necessary if he were to be ordained into the Church.

'His father wants him to join the Church but does he? What do you think, Millie?'

For her part, Mildred found James charming if unsettling. It was his questions; they were direct and piercing. While they made her uncomfortable, she was also aware she welcomed them. Talking to him seemed to draw her out of herself. James assured her he was fascinated to find out more about the years that she and William lived abroad.

'I understand you made sketches of places you visited. William says you draw very well,' James said. They were in the conservatory. Mildred was showing him the lemon and orange bushes she had grown from seed. James opened one of the windows; the place was airless. The boy added: 'William says you made drawings of churches, how they were decorated and so on. I wondered ... might I see them?'

Mildred stiffened. 'I've not shown my drawings to anyone apart from William.'

'Perhaps you've not met anyone else who was interested in seeing them before. But I am,' James persisted.

She was taken aback. 'I'm not sure ...' she muttered, and split off brusquely, walking out into the garden. His comments felt intrusive. She did not know why but she felt disconcerted.

She sat on a bench by the pond. Edged with day lilies and ferns, the water followed the curve of the wall, and she could feel reflected heat from the bricks. Fish turned lazily beneath the green surface of the water. A wood pigeon gave a hollow call. A few minutes later, James came over to where she sat.

He stood for several moments without speaking. Then he

said quietly: 'I'm sorry if I've upset you, Mrs Holland. I'm interested, that is all.'

For a time, neither spoke. Then James said: 'You mentioned wanting to set up a studio here. Well, I've found the perfect place.'

# 8

She found herself dressing a little more carefully each day; choosing a brooch which picked out the colour of her eyes and changing her day collar for a lace one for supper, habits she had given up in the last few years. What was she thinking of? She felt almost guilty as she realised that she now looked forward to the times when she could talk to James, ask his opinion. Was it wrong to enjoy someone's company? She had been lonely since coming to Huntingfield, and here was someone to talk to, someone who wanted to know what she had done. It felt like a long time since anyone apart from William had shown an interest in what she did or thought. And William was often distracted, thinking about his work.

It was this attention which finally persuaded her to bring out her sketchbooks. She and James had been sitting in the parlour one afternoon. Despite it being June, the wind blew in bursts and rose petals clung to the wet grass. 'I've not had the chance to travel,' he said. 'I would love to see the world.'

'Perhaps you will have the chance after Oxford.' She threw open the window for it was clammy in the house.

'I don't think so. I must start training for the Church as soon as I complete my studies. My father cannot afford to support another son. Philip is trying for a seat in Parliament and it's costly. I must start earning a living as soon as I can.'

It seemed ungenerous not to share her good fortune with this intelligent young man. He might never have a chance to visit Europe or Asia Minor. But her legs were reluctant to climb as she went upstairs to fetch her sketchbooks. She crouched down to drag out a tatty leather tote from under the bed. Dust tickled her nose. Inside the bag were bundles of drawings tied together with raffia and ribbon as well as cardboard folders of watercolour paintings. What shall I show him? Mildred felt acutely embarrassed that someone would now see her efforts, these private intimate offerings.

Did James like them or was he being polite? He sat on a low chair balancing a sheaf of drawings on his knee, his dark hair falling forward, his long fingers curled gently around the curling edges of the paper, and a thought flashed through her: she wanted him to touch her body in just this way. Horrified, she flushed and turned away.

'What is this animal doing?' he asked, looking up. She was grateful he could not see inside her head or hear her thumping heart. Swallowing hard, she told him about the patient beast who must walk in circles every day to grind palm oil. And as they talked for the rest of the afternoon, it was as though they had drifted far away from the Suffolk rain; in her vivid descriptions, they were together in hot and strange places.

'My love, it is wonderful to see you looking so cheerful. It must be our young visitor!' said William with a broad smile. They were getting ready for bed. It had been warm all day. Mildred stretched out on the bed in her chemise, moving the air with a feather fan.

'Or perhaps it's our new bath?' he said proudly. 'Wonderful to splash water straight out of the tap, don't you think? Comforted my hot legs today. Move over, my dear.' William wiggled a space for himself on the bed beside her. 'How is James getting on, do you think? Is he doing his reading? He's not as focused on his work as his father would wish. I do hope he passes his exams.'

'I'm not sure he really wants to go to Oxford,' she said lazily, her eyes closed. Her heart gave a little skip.

'No doubt he will do as his father wishes. And then he will be ordained.'

'Perhaps he won't.'

'But he must, surely?' He was definite. 'James must complete his education and then find himself a living. Sydney cannot afford to fund James as well as the older boy, not once he leaves Oxford. He must make his own way.'

'He wants to make his own way, not his father's!' She sat up and glared at her husband. 'He does not want to join the Church. Life may be straightforward for you, William – and people like you, who never question what's expected of them!' She almost spat out the words. 'But it's not the same for everyone. Some people cannot accept what they are expected to do and they won't do it. Why should they, after all?'

William looked perplexed. 'Of course, Millie, of course. Calm yourself, my love. You know James, you know him better than I do. You've been talking to him. Perhaps you're right? I was only saying what I know his father wants.'

Mary was anxious about going to new places, Rose knew that, but she would still suggest it. 'You can come, Mary, now you've got the baby.' It was the week before the Hollands' summer party when all the children of the village and their parents were invited to the Rectory. It was Sunday evening. Rose was helping her sister, collecting the dry washing off the line in Mary's back yard. Her husband, Seth, was working away again.

'Won't know no one,' said Mary suspiciously. 'What would I do?'

'All the other village women with little ones will go. Bessie can go in for the bonny baby competition, watch the paper boats sail on the pond. She'll love it,' Rose urged, 'and there's marvellous food, things you never usually have. And I told you about the gentleman staying at the Rectory, didn't I? James Pegler. He'll be there.'

Mary disappeared into the cottage and returned with a bucket of scraps for the pig. Rose watched her sister lean over the fence to throw them into the sty and to scratch the pig's back with a stick as the animal grunted and fed.

'Don't know how you do that,' Rose shivered. 'Making friends with a creature, knowing you'll be killing him months later.'

'You'll be eating ham and sausages just like the rest of us, Rose.'

'I know, I know ... So, will you come?'

'You've mentioned that gentleman a few too many times for it not to mean something,' said Mary. 'You keen on this James then?'

'You're teasing me, Mary. The gentleman is from a good family. But if I'm honest, I think I catch him looking at me sometimes, out of the corner of his eye. Like he likes what he sees.' Rose giggled.

'Hum, does he? Well, watch out for any man and keep him

looking, that's my advice,' said Mary darkly. 'None of 'em stick around once they've got what they want. Didn't tell you, Rose but I think I'm pregnant again. I'll be too tired to come to the Hollands' *party*.' Mary almost spat the word.

Rose remembered how bleak Mary became weeks after her first child Bessie was born; forgot to dress herself or the baby, was distracted, even abusive when Seth reminded her she must feed the baby. In the end Rose paid a neighbour to wet-nurse Bessie until Mary came to her senses. It was frightening. Didn't help the marriage neither.

'Thought Seth was working away now?' said Rose.

'Yea, mostly. But it don't take no man long to make his presence felt, as you might put it. Seth comes home for a meal, clean clothes and ... things happen. You don't know about *that*. Best you know nothin' ...'

'Don't treat me like a child, I know what you're talking about.'

'Lucky for you, you don't though.' Mary's expression was hard to fathom.

On Saturday after lunch, the children's party began. First there were running and sack races in the field near the Rectory, then each child took a turn on the swings. Ropes had been fixed to the lower boughs of two old trees, and William and Mr Gould, the schoolmaster, pushed each child as high as they could fly; screams of delight and fear echoed around the Rectory garden walls. Red-faced children raced paper boats on the pond, their cheeks puffed out with the effort of blowing them across the water, and in the end every child was found to have won a prize, even if it was only for being there.

Tea began. Rose, Thomas and Cook set out the food on long

trestle tables and spread sheets on the grass for picnicking. Chicken pieces, cheese rolls, pork pie, scones and cake were washed down with lemonade and ginger beer, then Cook handed out little dishes of iced cream.

Mildred watched from the shade. 'We do enjoy giving this party,' she said to James who strolled up to join her. 'And William is so good with the children.'

Both watched as William rescued one of the boats stranded among the water lilies in the pond and handed it triumphantly back to a little wailing girl. He didn't seem to care that his sleeve was dripping with water.

Neither spoke. The silence was awkward. Finally, she said lightly: 'Oh look at that little boy, stuffing cake into his pockets. It'll turn to crumbs!'

The party roiled on before them. How grateful Mildred was to be able to summon a smile, to paste the expression of pleasure across her face which otherwise threatened to break into pieces. Foremost in her mind was the knowledge that James was leaving Huntingfield the following day. Due to be up in Oxford for the entry examination in a few weeks' time, he was riding back to his family in Essex. James would not be at their meals any more or share her daily walk or amuse her with tales of the previous day's lesson. How was it that within only a matter of weeks he had become part of the fabric of her life? He would go up to Oxford and might be too busy to visit. She might not see him again – ever.

She could not hold it back. She blurted out: 'I shall miss you, James.'

Her words were heavy, laden with meaning, but when she sensed he was looking at her, she did not meet his gaze. She could not. She was frightened she would break. In between the shouts of the children playing, there was a terrible silence.

Desperate to break it at last, she said as defiantly as she could: 'We will *both* miss you.'

Help me Lord to maintain a semblance of convention, she prayed. Her legs felt weak but she forced herself to stand. 'Help me hand out pennies and sweets to the children as they leave, will you?'

# 9

1855 AUTUMN

I t was always good to be going home. William glanced out of the trap as it jogged him along the last few isolated miles as the road dipped towards Huntingfield. It was grey and wet, a very ordinary autumn day, but a happy one for shortly he would be with his dear wife. After twenty years of marriage, he still looked forward to seeing her. He imagined finding her in their bedroom and her walking towards him with that half smile, circling her arms around his waist, pressing her heavy breasts into him and burying his nose in her hair, her familiar, musky scent.

But in his heart, he knew all this was unlikely. For the last year, Mildred had 'been low' as he put it to himself, or 'not herself' when he spoke to her. Not all the time, it was true, but particularly in the darker months of the year, her moods were unpredictable. If he was away for a night or two, he might return to find her in bed, lying in a darkened room, a cold flannel on her forehead. Rose would confirm that Mrs Holland had rarely left the bedroom and eaten little. At other times, she became excitable, took day-long walks, returning with mud-streaked skirts. She would stay up late, insisting one of the Rectory rooms needed redecorating, send a flurry of letters to London for samples and swatches, only to abandon her plans days later. Her sleep was disturbed. She would complain of sudden rushes of heat.

And she had not become pregnant. Despite the settled life of Huntingfield which they hoped would result in a conception, their prayers had gone unanswered. Mildred would be forty next birthday. The doctor had privately advised him that women going through 'the change' often became unsettled, even hysterical. As the trap swung through the gates, he gave a prayer that today she would be the cheerful Mildred he had married, the Mildred he still loved whatever her mood.

'She's down the garden,' said Rose as she opened the door.

Her face was grave but that was not unusual.

'In this rain?' William walked straight through the house and out of the back door. There she was sitting on a bench by the far wall, a cloak and hood pulled up over her head as the rain teemed down.

'Millie, hallo my dearest, what are you doing out here?' He hurried over and took her bitten fingers into his own to rub some warmth into them.

'William, you're back,' she spoke quietly from within the hood. 'Oh, I am well. I just needed some fresh air. I wanted to sit in the garden.'

He looked around. Most of the leaves had fallen from the trees and the lawn was strewn with soggy brown heaps. Dying foliage bedraggled the flower beds. A single pink rose clung to the stem, droop-headed.

'Any news?' He touched her shoulder. She shook her head.

'I'm getting wet here, Millie. Let's get back inside, eh? It's tea time,' and taking her arm firmly, he led her back into the house. Later, he called the household for evening prayers. Rose and Cook filed into his study, followed by a giggling Thomas. Rose nudged him in the ribs. Mildred, William and Thomas stood on one side, the women on the other. William began with some prayers and then nodded. Thomas pulled himself to his full height; all of five foot, he held his Bible up so high his chin was raised. Haltingly, he read out a psalm. Rose and Cook stared straight ahead, not daring to look. Only one whispered prompt from William and the reading was complete. There was a palpable air of relief as everyone joined in with the Lord's Prayer and a grateful 'Amen'.

'Thank you Thomas, that was well done,' said William as the servants trooped out: the boy was pink with success.

'He is doing very well with his reading; I am quite proud of him.' William pulled up a chair so Mildred could sit by the fire. 'You've done well to teach him.' She looked directly at him for the first time since he'd arrived home. She seemed calmer, somehow more settled. Perhaps it was the service, he thought. 'How have you been, my dear?' he said.

'It's been quiet. I've been sewing.'

'I called in on the Hammants on the way home to see how John is getting on. You'll be pleased to hear he's much better. The stump is healing well and he's using crutches. He's got plans, he was telling me. He's designing a moving contraption, fixing old barrow wheels to the seat of a chair so he can get about. Harry Browne's boy, Timothy, is helping him. Millie?'

She was staring into the fire, nibbling at a nail, her expression distant and sad. He still found her beautiful; her thick reddish hair, freckled skin and high cheekbones. He watched her. He felt defeated when she wasn't happy. He feared his natural enthusiasm sometimes irritated her and his clumsy attempts at jokes probably had the same effect but he was driven to try to make her more cheerful.

'John says he will use the chair to push himself about – isn't it a marvellous idea? Then he won't have to use crutches. He'll be able to chop the wood, not balancing on one leg, and then bring it as far as the back door of the cottage. He's keen to take a burden off Sally; she's had to do everything since the accident.'

'That's good news,' she nodded.

'It's very hard on them though. They take the parish allowance but I still think they'll decide to take the eldest girl out of school so she can start work.'

'They need the money ...'

'But she needs an education!' He sighed. 'I told them I would give them a bit if they let her stay on at school. But they're not sure ...'

They both knew John was considered hard-working and dependable. The manager at Heveningham Hall had paid him extra money in the past to act as the foreman for a team of men when things were busy. John had probably assumed he would have employment for the rest of his working life. He might even have banked on putting a bit aside for old age. But now the Hammants were struggling to survive day-to-day.

William sighed. He had been left a generous annuity from the same uncle who bought him the living of Huntingfield, and as the Rector, he also received an annual tithe from the parish.

It meant that while he and Mildred were not wealthy, they were comfortable financially. They both felt it was their duty to be generous in the parish and to do what they could to ease financial and other problems that burdened local people.

William knew he had been spending too freely recently. Paying for the schoolhouse to be built, employing the Goulds as the schoolmaster and wife, buying property in the village to provide cheap rented accommodation for local people and now the renovations at St Mary's.

'There must be something else we can offer John.' William stood up. 'Now, I must write and thank the Bishop for the

73

splendid dinner. There was a fascinating discussion about capitalism and faith, Millie, you'd have enjoyed it.'

He was about to leave when Mildred said, 'I had a letter from James yesterday. He says that he's going to finish his degree. Another one of your successes.' She glanced up at William. 'As for ordination, he is not so clear. I wonder if he can stand out against his father's wishes. Sydney is a difficult man to refuse.'

'Sydney was in Norwich and told me as much. This suggestion that James might not go through with ordination ... well, he was furious! Sydney wants me to do what I can to dissuade James. I'm not sure I have much influence with him though. Perhaps you have more, Mildred? I know you got on well.'

She looked away. 'I'm not the best person to talk to James. Anyway, I'm not sure I would try to dissuade him from doing what he wants. He knows his mind, and if the church is not for him, I for one would not try to persuade him to become part of it. He must find his own way.'

Mildred left early for the village. Children swarmed up the lane on their way to school, a sea of chattering boys and girls. The crowd parted, went quiet as she passed through, and then returned to a full-throated roar. Beyond the village, she cut through a gap in the bushes shuttered with branches and went into a wood, picking up a path that led away from the stream. The autumn leaves crunched satisfyingly underfoot as she threaded through a line of tall elm trees. Rosehips hung like drops of blood from branches. She scraped the skin from the orange-red fruit with her teeth, tasting the sour-sweetness.

In the deep silence of the wood she opened her letter from James. It always gave her a thrill to receive an envelope with his writing on it, even though she was usually disappointed with its contents. Each time he'd written in the last two years, his news was much the same: parties and lectures he'd attended, his quandary about what to do with his life, his desire to leave the country and to try his luck in the colonies, his quarrels with his father. She was not sure what she was hoping to read. All she knew was that the contact always left her unsettled. It stirred up feelings of regret, of possibilities, of loss. She missed his company and his interest in her work and his youth. And, if she was honest, his presence too; it had wakened feelings in her, feelings of longing that made her breathless.

When James first left the Rectory, it had been terrible. Every morning when Mildred woke, he was the first thing she thought about and when she closed her eyes at night, his wide dark eyes floated before her. Much more terrible than that, though, was when she lay with William. It would flick through her mind that it could be James whose tentative fingers stroked her thigh, whose tongue traced the curve of her waist. These thoughts were shocking, terrible, and she twisted with guilt until she could summon the civilised part of her mind to drive away those devilish thoughts. But the deep pleasure they created could not be denied. Replete with satisfaction, she was tainted with remorse.

Mildred did not feel like that now. She was strong again. It was true that she had never stopped loving William, even when James was in her mind. Now James's letters merely stirred up uncomfortable memories as well as disappointment with herself. How could she have been so weak?

Mildred folded the paper away carefully. There were still some blackberries on a bush and it was a relief to stretch out her arms and pick the few that looked juicy. She was drawing patterns of entwining leaves, fruits and flowers, thinking to design a border for church kneelers. Her plan was to find village women who were good at embroidery and employ them to make up the covers; also to engage others to upholster the kneeler frames. Mildred was pleased with this idea. But what about employment for the men? William told her about Tom Fake the wheelwright whose family business had been in Huntingfield for over a hundred years. Orders were dwindling because machines were taking over the traditional craft of wheel-making. The situation was so bad, said William, that the Fake sons had left the village for work in the North, leaving their parents behind. Who could blame them? Everyone in the village was suffering.

## 10

1857 SPRING

William returned to the Rectory, his face pink with excitement. He almost bounced into the parlour where she was sitting by the fire and kissed her, his wispy hair swaying like spun sugar. He had been in Norwich at the regular monthly meeting held for all the clergymen in his diocese.

'I met such an interesting man, Millie! Edward Blackburne, an architect from London. The Bishop has engaged him as the Diocesan Surveyor of Norwich. I've told you his plans; the Bishop is determined that the churches in his county should be renovated. So many, like St Mary's, have fallen into disrepair and he wants us to make improvements. But more than that, and I am in total agreement with him, he wants the remodelling to be in the Gothic style. And this is Edward Blackburne's speciality. Yes, indeed! He's very well known in London for remodelling churches in the Gothic style and we had a fascinating ...'

As he stood by the fire, his eyes shining in the light as he chatted on, Mildred reflected on how she sometimes found William's boyish enthusiasm draining. But tonight she was amused by his eager talk.

'We could invite him to dinner, Millie.'

'Why on earth would he want to come all the way from Norwich to dine with us?'

'He lives in London some of the time – that is where his practice is – and he visits Norwich when the Bishop demands. But Edward will soon be very local. He has been commissioned to renovate St Edmund's church in Southwold, only some thirty miles away, and he will be working there for several months. I am sure he would like to come for dinner at Huntingfield. Shall I ask him?'

William's eagerness for Edward Blackburne was not reciprocated. Edward had been singularly unimpressed by William. Introduced to him by the Bishop, within minutes Edward decided William was a well-meaning but dull man, one who acquiesced to his superiors because he lacked the independence of mind necessary to forge his own ideas. Edward rarely changed his mind, even if the facts suggested he should. But few can resist the flattery of another's interest. When William sought Edward's views on the best way to renovate a roof, Edward was gratified to see his advice was received with studied enthusiasm. Edward had gleaned from hints dropped by the Bishop that William had inherited from a generous uncle. He would be able to consider a substantial renovation of his parish church, St Mary's in Huntingfield and Edward was determined to secure the commission. He left William with the firm impression that they had begun a warm and fruitful relationship.

The son of a small town clerk and a barmaid, Edward Blackburne had done well at school. His parents were determined their son would rise in the world and his father paid a local engineering firm to take him on as an apprentice. It was here Edward received a useful background in technical drawing as well as an exposure to the art and science of architecture. It was not common for such a person to rise to the eminent profession of architecture. But few possessed the single-minded determination of Edward Blackburne. He worked with an ambition that frequently made his work colleagues uncomfortable. When the man in charge of designing a small municipal building caught influenza and died, Edward stepped forward, some felt with unseemly haste, to ask if he could take on the job. Edward cared not a fig if his colleagues didn't like it. His career as an architect had begun.

All day long there were raised voices and crashing pans in the kitchen. Footsteps clattered up and down the corridor. William was trying to marshal his thoughts for Sunday's sermon but each time a pithy idea came into this mind, some noise would disturb him and it would float away. Usually he found interruptions frustrating and would complain to the servants. But today he decided to ignore it all. William positively welcomed the disturbance because it signified something out of the ordinary. The Hollands were giving a dinner party. William stayed at his desk, smiling at the empty page.

'Let us make it a proper event,' he had said. 'I shall invite Mr Blackburne and our friends Richard and Mrs Owen, and I will ask Sydney Pegler as well. He may have news of James. That should make a good party, what do you say, Mildred?'

She did her best to appear pleased. How different her reaction was, he thought, from that of the enthusiastic young woman he had courted and married. Spirited, at times exhausting, Mildred as a young woman had always been keen to meet new people, full of questions, friendly and bubbly. The woman who faced him now seemed preoccupied.

By mid-afternoon, Cook's usual calm had turned to shouts.

Then Rose came to his study, fearful she might drop the food on the floor when serving the guests.

'It's no good. Let's go for a walk, Millie. Leave this bedlam for a while!'

They went to the church. There had been many improvements made over the last nine years. All the cracked window glass had been replaced and there was new stone tracing around the windows. The roof was watertight and the walls were painted white.

'I'm pleased with the oak pews. Now the parishioners can sit comfortably,' said William. 'It's dry and clean. My dear, we've made a fine start, there's no doubt about that. St Mary's is a simple place but one of which I am proud. But I remain convinced, and I have the Bishop's support in this, that people would be helped towards a deeper faith, a deeper sense of the glory of God, if it were more ... splendid! I'm determined to do more.'

She wandered down the aisle and sat on the pew in the chancel designated for the Hollands. A lion, carved in wood, reared up dramatically from the armrest. She stroked its smooth head. Through the plain glass window over the altar, the clouds rolled by.

'Remember the stained glass we saw in Italy?' Mildred sighed. 'Those wonderful windows, biblical tales in shimmering colours. It would be wonderful to have stained glass here. It's costly I know.' She reached out to touch his arm. 'I miss our travels, so very much, William. All those places we saw together, learning and seeing and ... Now you are busy with the parish and the school, and I am ...' Her voice trailed away.

'Did I not tell you, Millie? Lady Huntingfield has offered to pay for a replacement for the east window in honour of Lord Huntingfield. It was malaria that killed him, you know.'

'Yes, it was terribly sad,' she murmured.

'I'll ask Edward if he can recommend an artist we can commission for the window. He'll know of someone.' He kissed the top of her head. 'As long as Cook and Rose stop quarrelling long enough for us to hold this dinner! I hear a carriage; it must be Sydney.'

~

William called the dinner a 'celebration of spring'. At first Mildred had found his plans annoying but spending the morning in the spring sunshine collecting hedgerow flowers for table posies had been agreeable. Then she decorated name cards for each guest's place. The dinner table, covered in a fine French linen tablecloth and dressed with lace napkins, polished silver and glassware looked inviting.

William had also insisted they must look their best. So the mothballs had been shaken from Mildred's blue satin dress, its ruffled sleeves and collar carefully pressed, her beaded shawl sponged and the pink brocade slippers and sequinned evening bag unpacked from layers of tissue paper. Ask Thomas to light the candles, she instructed Rose as she dabbed scent behind her ear. Was that the Owens at the door?

The meal was splendid, she later congratulated Cook. The savoury soup, jellied terrines and roasted pigeon were declared delicious by everyone. None of the guests were served food in their laps. Mildred nodded proudly as Rose came in with a tray of candied fruits, her face flushed with all the fetching and carrying.

Mildred looks happy, William thought. She was clearly enjoying being the hostess.

'Now what will you have? Lemon pudding, and we also have preserved fruit with syllabub. Mr Blackburne, I mean Edward!' and she gave him a gracious smile.

They began to talk of his restoration work at St Edmund's.

Edward enjoyed being the centre of attention.

'Almost complete, I'm glad to say. The roof has been restored and the ceiling will be finished soon. The commissioners are content so I am pleased.'

'I understand you are a leading specialist in medieval art, Mr Blackburne?' Ann said. With her dark hair falling in ringlets on either side of her face and a blue-spotted dress setting off her slender figure, Mildred saw a new side to her friend, a charming woman who knew how to flatter a man.

'You are very kind, Mrs Owen, I am sure. I have some reputation that is true. I've been privileged to work in many parts of the country where I must accept that my expertise is indeed appreciated.' He sat a little straighter. 'At present, I am working at St Edmund's in Southwold, and a very fine place it is too.' Edward turned graciously toward William. 'I am hoping that our hosts will be kind enough to visit me there. Perhaps you and Mr Owen might also be interested in seeing the work?'

'That would most enjoyable and a privilege, no doubt,' Ann said graciously. 'Thank you for the invitation. I have a great interest in the decorative arts. I studied as an artist myself and worked for some years; before I married, of course.'

This was a surprise to Mildred. A drip of syllabub fell from the serving spoon she was using on to the tablecloth. Absentmindedly she reached out to dab it and licked her finger, staring at her friend in amazement.

Edward said, 'A particular interest, may I ask?'

'I specialised in stained glass, mainly. There were some commissions, domestic and ecclesiastic which I accepted ... before coming to Suffolk.' Ann's cheeks were flushed.

'I declare, this area is full of talented women!' Edward smiled gallantly at them both. 'And you, Mrs Holland. William tells me you have a flair for drawing and painting, that you did a lot of work when you lived abroad.'

'Well, I wouldn't say talent ... I did enjoy sketching, very much as an amateur, of course. Ann, you never mentioned you were an artist!'

'It didn't seem relevant, Mildred. I haven't done anything like that in the last few years, not since we came to the vicarage. I have the children now. It's something I did in my past.'

'Yes, all the in past now,' Richard Owen, Ann's husband finally spoke. He clearly enjoyed his food for he'd eaten solidly through the courses, had said almost nothing apart from 'yes, please, I will,' and 'would you like the salt?'

He added, 'Now Ann is at home with the girls, and we both agree that this is the rightful place for a wife and a mother. No need for her to work. With the girls to look after, the servants, the house, her birds.' He turned to Edward. 'Blackburne, I understand much of the stained glass in churches in this area was destroyed during the Reformation. Is that so?'

Mildred had never seen this side of Richard. A bookish, quiet man, she had assumed he acquiesced to his more spirited wife but she had just witnessed a hard steely side.

'A vandal by the name of Dowsing, William Dowsing, a puritan living around here was the main perpetrator,' Edward was in full swing. 'During the Civil War, he was commissioned by Cromwell. He visited about a quarter of parish churches in the county, destroying stained glass windows, crosses, icons as he went. In some areas, he got local people to do his work for them – and then charged them a third of a pound for his services!'

The guests laughed. Mildred saw Ann didn't join in; once animated, she now looked preoccupied.

William said: 'Our church was desecrated even earlier than that. The parish records show that in 1583 the church was whitewashed to remove paintings and other decorations on the walls. Which you can shall see for yourself, Edward. We will show you in the morning.'

'Many Cambridge University College churches were damaged in the same purge,' Sydney was flushed from drink or the heat. 'Yet it was in Oxford that the movement in which William and I are so involved first started. The Gothic revival, the only true style of Christian architecture, is the way forward, I tell you! It will bring people back to Church. That's our view and I'm sure you agree, Mr Blackburne!'

Why is Sydney so irritating? Mildred thought. She wanted to flick his ear. He was shiny somehow, like a marble. She heard him mention James.

'Yes, he's about to come down. James is a headstrong boy, got some half-baked plans to leave for India. To work for a tea company or some other outfit, he doesn't seem very clear. I'm not pleased, not at all. You couldn't have a word, could you, William?' He stared hard at his host as though he could force him to comply with his request. 'Try to dissuade him, would you? I really feel he is throwing away a very good opportunity to chase a boyish dream.'

'I tried last term, mentioned it to him. He's a very impressive young man, Sydney. We very much enjoyed it when he stayed here, didn't we, Mildred? '

Mention of James's name always made her feel uncomfortable. She stood up. 'Indeed we did, Sydney, a fine young man. Now excuse us, gentlemen. We ladies will leave so you may smoke.'

Ann stood by the drawing room window. The curtains were open, a bright moon suspended just above the treeline.

'Thank you for a wonderful evening, Mildred, I have enjoyed myself.'

'Did you really? And what about the pompous Mr Pegler?

An old friend of William's, he's very fond of him. Fierce about his son, don't you think? Sydney wants James to do exactly what he's told. You know William tutored him for his exams.' Mildred shrugged. 'If there was one way to put his boy off the Church, it was coming to live with William and me! So quiet and dull. Now, you mysterious woman, why have you never mentioned your past as an artist. Why?'

'There's nothing much to tell you really.' Ann continued to gaze at the garden. 'I studied for a few years, became interested in an artist called Samuel Palmer; do you know his work? There were one or two commissions I took on. I enjoyed it very much but it became ... I was never going to be ... Anyway, I met Richard, and I gave it all up.'

Such a strange emotionless tone. Mildred couldn't see her friend's face; it was hidden by her curls which had started to droop.

After a moment, Ann spoke again: 'All in the past, anyway. So, my daughter Sarah! Thank you for rescuing her poor little finger from that nasty wasp sting. You're very nimble with the needle.'

Mildred sensed the conversation about Ann's past was closed, at least for the time being.

The next morning, Mildred walked with Edward to the church. Spring light filtered through the plain glass windows, lighting up the interior. She set a vase filled with flowers on the altar, and watched as her guest wandered around the church.

'So much of the so-called superstitious imagery in Suffolk's parish churches – paintings, angel roofs and so on – was destroyed even before Dowsing. Can you see the evidence of whitewashing just there?' Edward pointed to an area of the wall.

'And I understand from William the parish records show there may have been murals too? A rood and screen, you can see from the wall damage there, and the destruction of religious artefacts, perhaps glass windows. All this can be restored – if that is what you decide you want.'

Mildred said: 'You can see where we've started. Mended the roof leaks, that sort of thing. But it's not been well received by some of the parishioners. There you are – village life! Some people hate change and they're suspicious of everything that's new, even if it's going back to the past. It makes it very hard.' Her face clouded. 'I find it exhausting to be frank.'

'I can see that you have a genuine interest, Mrs Holland.'

For the first time she looked at the man her husband admired so keenly. Edward was short with a swarthy complexion. His intense stare was disconcerting; he stood a fraction too close as though he expected to find something there and would keep looking until he did. 'If you would care to visit Southwold, I would be pleased to show you what we're doing. Your husband indicated you and he might consider a short holiday by the coast?'

Mildred felt uncomfortable, as though he had seen inside her. She moved away to escape his gaze; pretended to arrange the altar flowers. How could she tell him how hard it was for her to be interested in anything any more?

'I am sure we would like to visit St Edmund's. That is most kind,' she said. 'And a trip to Southwold. Perhaps. I will speak with my husband about it.'

# 11

They were given a large bedroom at the back of the inn. As soon as the maid shut the door, William lay back on the bed with a sigh.

'Come and join me, wife!' She found his playful tone irritating.

'I want to walk by the beach.'

'We're on holiday. We have all afternoon.'

'I'm tired, William. Not in the mood.'

'Love in the afternoon, don't you remember, our favourite time?' Caressing her hands, he tried to coax her on to the bed. 'Why do you pick at your lovely fingers?' he teased.

She pulled away and placing her hat on the washstand, caught sight of her face in the mirror. 'My hair's in disarray. I must pin it again at the back. Look at your middle-aged wife.' She frowned. 'We're by the sea, we should walk. And then tomorrow we'll see your funny friend Mr B and I'll be a cheerful wife.'

The Swan was a public house. The bar was crowded with faces, shiny with heat and drink and conversation, men enjoying themselves. It was what she needed, she decided, a change of scene. It was what she loved while they were travelling, hearing strange languages and trying to work out what people were saying. Other people's conversations always sounded fascinating. It was foreign enough here, she realised; she could barely understand the men's accents.

She and William sat in a pretty parlour, low-ceilinged with comfy chairs and little tables where tea and scones were served. She longed to walk but William was always hungry when on holiday so they chose a table and ordered. She half-listened to his chatter. 'I met him, the Mayor. Very forward thinking. He and some local businessmen are pressing the railway company to extend the line right into Southwold town centre. They'll have to find some of the money, of course.' She declined as he took another slice of cake. 'A train would bring a lot of employment into the town, and more visitors, too.'

When he had finished, they set off along the High Street to Gun Hill which rolled down in a sweep of green grass to the cliff edge. Steep steps dropped down to Sole Bay beach. A pale sun lit up the grey sea as it swelled like a breathing beast. Small fishing boats leaned up on the shingle and a few fishermen mended nets and stacked boxes. Further down the beach, children played. The soft hiss of waves, breaking and sucking on the stones, mingled with the screech of seagulls. She breathed in the fresh fishy smell and felt tears prickle.

'This way, Millie.' She was glad he had not noticed, and they started to meander along the promenade. Along the beach as far as the harbour, there were people, working and moving and being. It was ridiculous but she almost felt jealous. Their lives were woven like leaves in a pattern, while hers was a flag that hangs limp on a still day.

'What a splendid scene. I think I like stone beaches more than sandy ones, do you?' He had barely stopped talking since they had arrived. 'Good to get away for a few days, see some new faces and places. A few suppers, some wine, a bit of shopping, that will do the trick.' He squeezed her arm. 'I know it can be hard living in Huntingfield. Quiet and peaceful, which I know we both appreciate, but for you, well, I suspect it can be a bit lonely at times. Especially since I'm so busy in the ...'

She stopped abruptly. 'Did you say "a bit lonely", William? Peaceful? Do you have any idea of what it's like for me? It's dead, William, do you hear me – dead!'

He was startled. 'That's a bit steep, surely? We knew we were coming to live in a village. I don't know what else you expected?'

'That's not what I mean. I know, that sounds terrible, it's ...' She turned away miserably. 'It's not Huntingfield, it's the life that I have there. It feels like there is nothing that I can *do*.'

'But it's what we'd always planned, Millie. To build up the congregation, bring them back to the faith, the cottage lectures are starting to interest people and the Bishop is very pleased that we're building a school ...'

'But that's your work, William! I'm hardly involved in any of it!'

'That's not entirely true. And we had a lovely supper party last month, you said so yourself.'

She tried to control her anger. 'Yes, we did. That is not what I'm talking about.'

'I ask for your advice all the time ...'

'And I am happy to give it,' she interrupted. 'I couldn't do my work without you.'

'This is hopeless. Do you not understand? I need to do more than run the house and speak to the servants! I'm bored, William!'

With an exasperated shrug, Mildred swung away from him and strode off along the promenade. William studied the waves. He was flummoxed. He knew his wife was dissatisfied and yes, it was sad for them both that she had not become pregnant. But surely they must obey God's will and willingly accept the path He chose for them? He remembered what John Holland his father-in-law said to him when he'd asked for her hand. 'Be warned that life with Millie will be interesting.'

It had seemed an odd thing to say at the time. Now William understood what his father-in-law had meant. The years they had lived abroad had been fascinating and different. Life in the Rectory was bound to be a little frustrating for Mildred by comparison. As for expectation, she struggled against it like a foal first broken for the bit.

Mildred was natural fast walker and anger chivvied her heels.

By the time he caught up with her, William was puffing. 'Mildred, please, wait.' He towered over her, his face blotchy with effort. 'I'm sorry, my dear, but what can I do?'

In a low voice, tense with restraint, she replied: 'I don't know … It's not clear to me either.' The breeze lifted her hat and she clasped it to her head. 'I can be happy at the Rectory, I know I can, and one day, I will. Huntingfield is where we belong. It's just, I don't know, I must find my *own* way to be there. I will play my part, help you as much as I can, but there must be something for me!'

A man reeled out of a nearby tavern, followed by raised voices. 'There are too many fishermen with not enough regular work to keep them busy.' William was relieved to talk of something different. 'The men end up getting drunk and causing trouble. The Mayor tells me there's a plan for a reading room; encourage these mariners to read and keep themselves busy.'

'We're all better when we're occupied, aren't we?' She laughed. And she accepted William's arm and they walked back into town, stopping in a little shop where she bought an amber hatpin for her sister and he bought her a brooch.

~

'Morning.' Rose averted her eyes from the man in blood-encrusted clothes outside the Fakes' cottage. The pig sticker was leaning on his killing stool, a long wooden wheelbarrow without sides on which the animal would be strapped helpless before having its throat slashed. His dirty fingers were wrapped around one of Mary's mugs. Rose was glad it was one of the chipped ones. 'Come to help, have ya?' the man looked her up and down. 'I can always use a strong lass, me. Even a stripling like you could hold on tight,' he leered.

Inside the cottage, Rose saw her sister had set a large pan of water on the range; another sat steaming on the earth floor. Mary barely looked up, only snapped: 'About time, girl, these children are getting under me feet. Give 'em this for breakfast, will ya?' She thrust Rose a bowl of congealing porridge and some spoons.

It was the squealing Rose hated more than the smell of the blood or the stink of carcass when a pig was killed and its guts were sliced open. But she reluctantly agreed that since the Rector and his wife were away for a few days in Southwold, she would look after the children, leaving Mary and Seth to help the pig sticker.

'Out me way!' Seth pushed past her with an armful of straw. He dumped the dried stalks on the ground near the pig killer's machine, then started to shape a golden mound. A pig bed. A place of eternal rest. A place of fire.

Rose called to the children: 'Bessie, Martin, Martha ... come over here to your auntie.'

The children huddled round her legs, dipping their spoons into the bowl's warm sludge, watching curiously as their father carried through another armful of straw. A piece of it floated down; Rose tickled Martin's chin.

'Ready for 'im now. Stand back, here he comes!' called Seth, and as the sty gate flung open, out barrelled the pig. Rose remembered it as a tiny piglet, pink as a finger, leaping around the sty with the joy of being alive. Even then she had sensed Seth and Mary salivating. Now, smelling food and freedom, the big animal powered towards the cottage on its sturdy legs, headed off by the pig man yanking on the slip-noose round its snout. Seth tugged on its tail to steer it from behind. Walking ham and blood pudding and sausages. Rose shivered.

'Shake that bucket, Mary, get 'im through that door!' shouted Seth, and with the rattle of acorns, the pig lumbered toward Mary who stood in the cottage doorway. As it entered the dark cottage, the creature seemed momentarily stunned and stood, transfixed, breathing heavily as though lost. Rose turned her head away as its wet snout snuffled her shoulder and the reek of pig filled her nostrils. She could not look, the guilt of knowing soon enough she'd been feasting on its flesh. Then the bucket's rattle attracted the pig's attention and it waddled its way on towards the door, shitting as it went.

'Hold 'im now!' the pig man barked. That's when the squealing began; high-pitched, panicky and desperate. The sound filled her head, made her ears ring. Rose gathered the children to her, squeezing their bony bodies to her tightly so their whimpers would cover the pig's dying cries. Then, as suddenly as it started, it was quiet. The children struggled out of Rose's grip and stood to watch through the door as their father traced the dead pig's body with a bundle of lighted straws. The terrible reek of singed hair filled the air as the creature's bristles were burnt off.

The three adults sweated and strained as they dragged the dead pig on to the pig sticker's stool. 'Close yer eyes if you don't want to see him stuck!' the pig man cried, and as a spurt of blood sprayed out, Rose hauled the children back down into her lap and buried her head in a tangle of limbs.

'He's gone. A good bleeder too. Look at this lot!' beamed Mary, staggering into the cottage with two buckets, her hands and skirt splattered red with blood. 'I'll be making a blood pudding now and once he's been hung a few days we'll joint 'im up. A bit for the pig sticker, sell some of the meat in the village, salt the rest for winter. With another babe on the way, I'm going to need it. Don't look so whimsy, Rose. Make us a cup of tea, you big sissy.'

After breakfast, William and Mildred left the hotel. It was chilly and they hurried along the busy high street, William in a scarf and Mildred with her hands in a muffler.

'Can you direct me to St Edmund's Church?' William asked.

A passer-by pointed the way.

It was a medieval church, a massive flint-walled building with a turreted porch, a tall bell tower and a steep copper roof over which men were scrambling like little ants. Workmen hurried in and out of the church with tools and materials; there was an air of urgency in the way they moved. William tapped the shoulder of a man.

'Is Mr Edward Blackburne about? Please tell him that Mr Holland and his wife are here to see him.'

They followed the man inside the church. Bright light poured in through the low set windows, setting off the vast stained glass altar window and sending coloured beams out along the patterned tiled floor. A carved wooden screen stretched across the vast interior, separating the congregation from the choir stalls. She noticed where the faces of saints on the painted panelling had been brutally scrubbed out leaving only faint outlines of feathered costumes and gold wings.

Looking up, they saw him, Edward Blackburne, some 90 feet high above their heads. He was standing with a group of workmen on frail wooden scaffolding. Above them arched a massive wooden hammer beam roof, decorated with panels of saints, flowers, fruits and gold rosettes. Mildred craned her neck to see him.

'He's flying, William, he's up there with the angels!'

For at the ends of some roof beams were fixed brightly-coloured crowned angels who smiled benignly at the world that milled beneath them, their feathered gold wings outstretched as though they were about to fly. Mildred stood mesmerised.

William took her arm. 'Edward has seen us! He's coming down.'

Edward started to climb down a series of ladders which connected the different levels of the scaffolding.

'Let's go and meet him.' William started to walk over to where the architect would reach the ground. He did not notice his wife had other plans. She had seen a ladder propped up on one side. Hesitating for only a moment before dropping her muffler on to a pew, she took hold of a wooden rung with one hand, raised her skirts with the other and started to climb.

'Mr Blackburne, I am coming!' Her face was bright with excitement. By the time William had hurried back towards her, she was on the fourth rung.

'Millie! Stop please, my dear, now!' he hissed, his voice urgent, his tone appalled.

She had reached almost his chest height. Looking down she could see the pink skin of his scalp through his thinning hair.

'What is it, William, I'm not frightened. You don't have to come.'

'No,' he whispered fiercely. 'It's not that! It's your dress,

Millie. People will be able to see under your skirts as you climb. And it's dangerous!'

She looked down at her husband in fury. His expression was partly beseeching, partly angry. She knew he was right, he often was. But was this a reason not to do what she wanted? From where she stood now, a man's height off the floor, she could see around the church. Few people had any interest in what she was doing. She started climbing again.

Then she felt the ladder start to shudder. Looking up, she could see the dark material of a trouser and a foot coming down towards her.

'Mrs Holland. Perhaps wait until I have come down myself? Then I can assist you,' she heard him say.

She had no choice, the man was blocking her ascent.

'All right, I'll get down.' It was hard to know where to put her foot as her skirts wrapped around her foot like wet fronds. Once back on the floor, she straightened her dress and glared at her husband.

Just then, two men walked by carrying between them the figure of an angel.

'Stop, please! Let me look.' She reached out to touch the carved face fringed with curls, the straight nose and full lips. Two upturned hands gave the Holy blessing. 'Oh, isn't it beautiful? It reminds me of a child, a beautiful innocent child.'

The carpenters stared at her, then muttered apologies and hurried on. It was all over in a matter of moments. Edward came over to them.

'Welcome, Mr Holland and Mrs Holland, it is a privilege to see you again. Thank you for your visit and my apologies for keeping you waiting ...' He shook William's hand, gave a short bow to Mildred and indicated they should proceed back down the church towards the door.

'There is something I must show you before Mrs Holland

has the chance to perhaps see the work for herself. I can ask the men to leave the church, William, and I'll go with her myself to ensure her safety. But first, let me introduce Southwold Jack.' He gestured toward the wooden figure of a soldier boy that stood by the font. 'As you can see, he is dressed in armour and holds an axe. This is used to strike a bell and to summon the congregation to worship. Visitors come from all over the country specially to see Jack. The Mayor says the town needs a train station so that more people can come to Southwold on their days out to visit him.'

'Just what I was telling you at tea, Mildred,' said William.

She was not listening. She was watching the angel statue being hoisted up the scaffolding by a rope, sacking unceremoniously wrapped around its body and face but still glorious as it rocked and swayed through the air as though flying free at last. She felt an absurd sense of happiness as the graceful carving reached the highest part of the church arriving where other angel figures were already set on the ends of roof beams. A workman gently manoeuvred the creature on to the beam and fixed it into position. Now the angel sat, high and proud, looking down on the humans scuttling beneath.

William was speaking: 'The Mayor is right. People want to travel these days so extending the train as far as Southwold would be a marvellous idea.'

William and Edward carried on discussing the advantages of steam travel for local business. 'And we found the carriage from Darsham was most uncomfortable. Didn't we, Mildred? Mildred?'

He turned to his wife. Her eyes were fixed firmly on Edward.

He had seen this expression before and he dreaded it. 'Mr Blackburne, we need your help,' she said.

'What do you mean, we need his help?' William winced. 'We

need angels at St Mary's, of course. Angels in the church – and Edward is just the man to help us.'

'Help you? What do you mean?'

'Can we rely on you, Mr Blackburne?' Mildred beamed. 'Please say we can!'

～

They walked back to the hotel. Her change of mood from yesterday was complete. She hung on his arm and chattered on about how marvellous it would be to have Edward to advise them on St Mary's. William barely listened. Her outburst in St Edmund's church had unnerved him utterly. She had tried to climb the ladder, what was she thinking of? And her anger on the beach! And now this suggestion to Edward Blackburne without consulting him. Her behaviour generally was becoming unpredictable and made him uncomfortable. He insisted she take a nap that afternoon and that he would walk around the town while she slept. When he returned an hour later, she was sleeping.

They had invited Edward to join them for dinner at The Swan. After a good meal and bottle of wine, Mildred seemed calmer. The architect explained they would be following East Anglian practice if they put angels on the ceiling arches of St Mary's.

'They were probably in your church originally. I've done some research and there was a puritan, Edmund Stubbs, who was the rector there very early on. It may have been him who destroyed the iconography and other features during the Reformation. But there's also evidence the whole county was strongly puritan so it may have been a gradual process of destruction.'

. . .

'You're the surveyor to the Bishop of Norwich, Edward? You're often away from London, then?'

'Yes, Mrs Holland. I advise the Bishop on all the churches in the diocese and I've worked in several churches, Ospringe and Westwell, for example. That does take me away from my main practice that is in London.'

His tone suggested he considered renovation work in Suffolk beneath him.

'It must be satisfying to be acknowledged for your work,' she said graciously.

'In the Bishop's view and no doubt yours also, Mr Holland, improvements such as we've discussed signify those high Church ideals to which we're all firmly committed. As a leading thinker in the field,' and he graciously inclined his head in William's direction, 'you will agree that ritual, ceremony but above all, beauty is the physical representation of Christianity.'

William was flattered. The man had a point. He would be following the Bishop's direction if he spent a little more money on St Mary's. He ordered brandy to be brought to the table.

'Go on, Edward, if I may call you that?'

'You could replace some of the plain glass windows with stained glass ...'

'That's a marvellous idea!' Mildred interrupted. 'Ann might be interested in taking the commission, you never know. She told us – do you remember, William – she used to make stained glass before she married?'

Edward nodded. 'It would be in keeping with the building and, of course, beautify the light. You could raise the chancel floor and use the medieval encaustic tiles to create that important distinction between the officiate and his flock.' Edward accepted a brandy.

'Lots of good ideas,' Mildred looked excitedly at William.

'Don't you agree, William? The villagers should be able to worship somewhere beautiful.'

William demurred. 'These suggestions appeal, I grant you. But we should concentrate on the school, Millie. I think I mentioned to you, Edward, we're having a new school built as well as a house for the schoolmaster. It's taking up a lot of my time – and money.'

Edward nodded.

'That's why you should let me organise it all!' said Mildred enthusiastically. 'We've talked so long about the sorts of changes that we want at the church; I do think we should start them as soon as possible. With Edward's guidance, of course,' she added hastily. 'I'll discuss all the ideas with you, William, but you wouldn't need to be involved every day. I would enjoy it so very much. It would ... it would suit me.'

'A joint project,' said Edward, looking from one to the other. William turned to Edward. 'Mildred and I travelled for many years in Europe. It did give us a marvellous opportunity to see the world.'

'Difficult then to adjust to life in one place, after so many years of following your interests?' Edward suggested.

'We have both found some aspects of village life more difficult that we at first imagined,' William said stiffly, fearful of Mildred's response.

'Difficult? We both love Huntingfield and its people! We're determined to do everything we can to bring faith and the love of the Lord back into the parish.' Mildred smiled. 'We will think more about your ideas, Mr Blackburne, won't we, William? Now, will you take more coffee?'

Mildred didn't raise the subject again until they had arrived back at the Rectory the following day. William's desk was piled with school building plans, a half written sermon for Sunday and unopened post. She knew this was her moment.

'I don't see why I shouldn't.'

He turned to his wife and was caught momentarily by her beauty. When passionate, her pale skin flushed at the throat and her nose glowed pink at the tip. It was as though she was lit from within. It had been a long time since he had seen her so invigorated.

'Edward left me a message at the hotel. He says he would only charge a small fee to act as our adviser.' She stood on tiptoe, pressed against him, brushed her fingers across his neck. 'We've talked so long, William, about the changes that we want at the church. I really think it would marvellous, I do! To start rebuilding St Mary's properly. With me in charge. It would give me something to occupy my time, and you are so busy with everything, William, you are. Do say yes!' She looked up, pleading.

There was a knock and Rose came in. 'Excuse me, but the builder is here to see you, Reverend Holland, something about the pipes at the school.'

'The new drainage system. I must get over there to see what they're doing,' he said, gathering his things hurriedly.

'Goodness, that is exciting,' she lied. 'Shall I come along?'

She followed her husband out of the house, slipping her arm through his. By the time they had walked down the long drive and reached the Rectory gates, she had his agreement. Mildred would be in charge of renovating the church in St Mary's of Huntingfield.

## 12

1858 SPRING

S he wrote to Elizabeth:
*I have been adrift for so long. The hours used to pass in a tedious roundabout. Now my days leave me giddy with excitement. After morning prayers, a kiss and smile, William goes one way and I another. I will tell you more as plans proceed – but it is exciting!*

She steps across the yard and climbs the stairs to a room above the stable block. It is long and low, the smell of horse and straw rising through the rough boards as the animals rustle and snort beneath her feet. Windows running along one wall show the distant back gardens of Huntingfield cottages, deep lanes shuttered with branches and the flat land of Suffolk. On a bright day, there is enough light for her to work without a lamp.

Robert and Thomas carry cast-off furniture from the Rectory – carpets, several chairs, a small sofa and lamps – and help her to arrange it. A long trestle table beneath the windows, a bookcase at the far end, a comfy chair, a table next to the stove and several lamps. Then the boys are dispatched to fetch her travelling trunks. They have stood in the attic, packed with mothballs and memories, neglected for the last ten years. Waiting for them to arrive is almost unbearable. She paces the room, adjusting a chair, straightening a cushion and springs to door while the boys stagger in with the booty.

'Yes, thank you, Tom, Robert, over here!'

The rest of the day is spent rifling through the artefacts she had collected when travelling. No wonder William had called her 'my magpie'. His face paled when told the cost of sending it all back to England, but agreed it would be a pity to abandon her treasures. How has she lived without them for so long?

She strokes the stone sculpture of a squat pregnant woman from Turkey, the ivory-inlaid table from Morocco, the carved red stool from the Levant, the ceramic urn from Greece. Around her are scattered metalwork bowls, keys, a jewel-encrusted filigree buckle, boxes of scented wood, painted icons, patterned tiles. Embroidered banners flutter from the beams. Swatches of satin in butterfly colours drape the furniture. She piles silky cushions and velvet pillows on a huge Persian carpet; sinks back on a sheepskin rug. These items would have looked inappropriate, garish even, in a home of a rector and his wife but in this hideaway, the foreign booty made an emporium of pleasure.

Finally, she has her room – or 'her studio' as James would have called it. How pleased he would be to see her here where she can think and plan and work.

And there is much that needs to be done to renovate St Mary's. She scrambles to her feet. She must make a list – several lists – of all the things that she and William have agreed must be built or improved.

Most mornings she works in the studio, running down to join William for lunch.

'You're being an angel, darling William!' She kisses him, 'and Edward is quite helpful, don't you agree?'

Once a week, the architect stays the night at the Rectory,

bringing pamphlets and brochures which describe processes and practices she had never known existed but are now becoming familiar. He always provided more detail that she needed (or wanted) when she asked him a question. But, she reminded herself, being thorough and precise were essential traits in an architect.

She writes to Ann:

*My dear,*

*You would find it hilarious to hear our talk at dinner – heating pipes and tile grouting are frequent topics! Mr Blackburne is quite the expert, and while he does provide an inordinate amount of detail which can be tedious in the extreme, nevertheless I know he will help me to do a good job. I am quite the clerk. I draw up lists and add all the costs for the work. William teases me but I know he is impressed with my attention to detail. He is gradually getting used to the idea that I can organise things as well as any man. Good news that baby Helen is starting to settle down. Send my love to the children ...*

A parcel arrived in the post. She recognised from the handwriting and the ceiling wax imprinted with his initials that it came from Edward. She carefully peeled off the thick brown paper to reveal a large book. Bound in soft black calf, it contained lithographic plates of saints, birds, animals and flowers taken from various medieval churches and buildings. The inscription read:

*To my dear friend Mildred in her quest to inspire a love of God through the love of beauty. A copy of my book. Edward Blackburne*

.   .   .

She had not known he was an author, too! She curled up on the sofa, wrapped in a paisley shawl William had bought for her in Vienna, and studied the book. Here was a man who not only appreciated art and beauty but understood the technical skills that underpinned it. His book, a tome really, not only contained stunning illustrations of work but also precise descriptions of the techniques used to produce them. The process of egg tempura painting used by artists for thousands of years to paint directly on walls. The cooking of rabbit's skin to make glue and the mixing in of whiting to create a smooth gesso surface. The beating of gold coins into paper-thin sheets to use in gilding. Lists of exotic artist's tools; hair of miniver, ermine and sable, knots of waxed silk binding vulture's quills, hog's hair bristles for brushes. Pigments carried thousands of miles on camelback. Every page revealed sorcerer's secrets. A rich and satisfying read.

'There is so much to do, my dear, my head is in a spin!' Mildred welcomed Ann into her studio. She had invited her to visit and to hear about 'an exciting development'.

Mildred cleared a space from the papers and journals littering the sofa. 'Apologies, I'm not looking after you properly. Sit down, please! I haven't shown you the beautiful book which Edward sent me. To give me ideas. What do you think?'

'It's quite a tome,' said Ann as she lifted the book on to her lap and started to flick through the pages. 'And you say that he wrote it and sent it as a gift? Kind of him. It is an impressive achievement, certainly.' Ann looked around. 'So this is your studio? And William has finally agreed you can be in charge of it all, the renovation and building? You are a lucky woman, Mildred.' Her tone was ambiguous.

'I have a little help! Edward is a treasure frankly. I write to him almost daily with questions. He must be irritated by me but never shows it. He tells me what needs to be done and then I do it. Actually, he's expected for tea any time now. There is something we'd like to ask you.'

Footsteps on the stairs announced his arrival. Ann watched as Edward almost bounced into the room. He didn't notice Ann sitting on the low sofa but made directly for Mildred, taking her hand and kissing it.

He said: 'My dear Mildred. And how are things going?'

'Very well,' she said, drawing her hand back firmly. 'Edward, you remember Ann Owen from our little supper party in the spring?'

It was clear Edward had not been aware someone else was present. He recovered himself quickly and made a low bow. 'Of course, Mrs Owen. Pleased to meet you again.'

Mildred could not contain her excitement. 'So are you ready, Ann? Steel yourself. Here's a big surprise, something we want to ask you.'

Mildred walked over to her friend. 'Will you take a commission for a stained glass window for St Mary's?' A reaction Mildred couldn't recognise washed over Ann's face. 'Paid for by money from Lady Huntingfield,' Mildred pressed on. 'The window's to be in honour of her husband's life. She wants it spent on a new altar window. And you will be the artist to make it!'

Ann remained silent.

'Have you nothing to say?' Mildred touched her shoulder. 'Ann?'

'It's impossible,' Ann shook her head. 'I can't do it, Mildred.'

'But ... if it's a question of needing somewhere to work ... Then what is the ...?'

Ann interrupted: 'How could I, with the children to look after? Please don't ask me. Not this, please!'

'We can find someone to help and there's no great rush ...'

'No, no!' Ann sounded exasperated and shook her head.

'You can work here. Set up a workbench, tools, anything you need!'

There was a brief pause, then Ann stood up, her eyes bright with fury.

'Why won't you listen to me, Mildred? I can't do it! I could *never* do it.' Quickly Ann gathered her things and pulled on her bonnet with a fierce tug. 'You don't understand, you don't listen Mildred! Thank you for thinking of me, it's kind of you, I'm sure. But it is simply out of the question. Can you hear that? Now, please excuse me. I must get back ... to the house ... to my children. Good day to you both.'

And she rushed out of the studio. Moments later, they heard the sound of a trap leaving the yard.

Mildred was dumbfounded. 'What an extraordinary reaction. I simply don't understand it. I thought she'd be pleased.'

She turned to Edward. He was unperturbed and was rifling through his briefcase. 'A disappointment, of course Mildred, but not a major problem.' He had found the papers he was searching for. 'Don't concern yourself. I know of another artist we can approach who will do it very well. He works in London. Look, here are his details.'

'For goodness' sake, Edward, I can't think of that now. My dear friend is upset. But I simply do not understand why!'

≈

Mildred didn't sleep well. Still smarting from Ann's outburst, she was also baffled by her reaction. Mildred had assumed Ann would be thrilled to have the work, excited by the prospect. People were unpredictable.

She decided not to mention the episode to William. After lunch, he left for the school building and she dragged a rug into the church and lay on it, wrapped up against the cold. She closed her eyes. She took herself back to Venice, one of her favourite cities. She remembered a ceiling that she and William had admired keenly and in her mind's eye she saw again, *The Martyrdom and Apotheosis of St Pantaleon*; the biggest canvas painting in the world. A huge cast of characters, magnified by *trompe-l'oeil*, exploded across the ceiling of this church depicting the saint's cruel death. It had taken the artist twenty years to complete the work. Legend had it that pure exhaustion caused him to tumble from the scaffolding to his death. Lost in thought, Mildred did not hear the door of the church creak as it opened.

'Busy at work I see.' Edward strode in. 'Hallo dearest Mildred.'

'Edward! You're not in Southwold?' She struggled to sit up, feeling guilty as though caught doing something forbidden. 'No, I've come to take you out for a little trip. We need to gather our ideas, to get inspiration. Recover from that little setback yesterday with Ann. Will you come?' And clicking his heels together, he bowed slightly. Holding out his hand, he helped her to stand.

She brushed herself down. 'Yes, why not. I must tell William though. He is across the lane at the school. I'll just go …'

'No need, Mildred. I took the liberty of calling in to see him myself. I told William that we are going out to visit some local churches, to research some ideas for the renovation project. He agreed it will be a useful outing.'

Edward drives the trap along the lane. She enjoys the ride,

feels the comforting pull and push of the horse's pace. The vast skies which sometimes suffocate her with their immensity, today offer freedom. Her eye follows the shapes of hedgerows, twisting and snaking through gaps between trees, then darting out to the distant horizon. Neither speak as they pound along the curving road, swinging and swaying down towards the wet marshland and hamlet of Blythburgh. There, set back from the road, stands the church. Like a queen on the edge of her watery kingdom, pools of wet and light bob round her skirts like loyal subjects.

Edward pulls the horse to a stop and jumps down from the trap. He offers his hand. Their eyes meet briefly and she sees how much he wants to please her. As they walk through the main door of the church, he catches her arm and gestures upward. High above, pinned like butterflies against the vast arching ceiling are delicate carved wooden angels with outstretched wings.

'Aren't they magnificent?' he whispers in her ear. 'They might be about to escape, to fly away.'

They stand suspended in the light which streams in through high windows casting illuminated patterns which dance on the opposite wall. The interior hums with crystal sunlight. A sense of joy washes through her as though she has never seen so intensely before.

'Wise and watchful, they look down on us poor mortals!' he murmurs.

She drifts around beneath them, spinning in slow circles. 'I've been thinking about them, Edward, ever since we visited you in Southwold. Now I see them again. Angels, I mean. I know our church is a modest little place, not so grand as St Edmund's or this church. But tell me – is there any reason – any *good* reason – why we shouldn't have them at St Mary's?'

The dark-suited, dark-haired man almost quivers with intensity.

'I can see no reason at all.' His tone is emphatic. 'It's a wonderful idea. There is the matter of cost, Mildred, but certainly the work can be arranged. There is a man I know, Mr Spall of Norwich, who can be commissioned to carve angels, or even to repair old ones. And he will fix them in position.'

'Good, yes, the cost. We will have to look into that. Oh, I've been looking at your book, Edward. I haven't thanked you properly for sending it to me. I'm enjoying it immensely.'

'Really? I'm flattered. Your interest in my work is most appreciated, as I am sure you know.' He is now standing very close to her; she can sense an energy that emanates from him. 'Yes, we can certainly arrange to have angels in your church. It would be a pleasure to work at St Mary's under your direction.'

Mildred says: 'I want *painted* angels.'

'Yes, yes, that can be arranged, too.' He looks at her, a half smile on his lips. She notices his teeth, small and slightly yellowed, and the thick moustache hairs that curl in at the corners of his mouth.

Then an idea forms in her head as clear as the bubble of saliva which glistens on his lapel. It is obvious. The travelling and the sketching, her unhappiness in Huntingfield, has been for a purpose. It will not be Edward who brings angels to St Mary's. It will be *her*.

Edward is blocking her way. Mildred brushes past him speaking quickly. 'It will be in the medieval style. William will agree, it's in keeping with his theological views. To have a beautiful church, decoration, colour, perhaps gold as well as colour. A real celebration ...'

Edward follows her along the aisle: 'Yes, we can find an artist to do this work. It will be difficult ... not impossible, expensive. It's a big task, take some time, even years to do something so extravagant ...'

'You haven't understood.' She stops walking and turns to face him. He almost bowls into her. 'I will do it. *I* will paint the ceiling.'

'You?' Edward splutters.

'Yes. I will paint it.'

'But Mildred, the ceiling is vast! It will take you years of cold, hard work.'

'I have the time, what is the problem?'

'... but working at a great height, off a high scaffold, reaching up to paint ... have you ever painted a fresco?'

She barely hears Edward's questions. A part of herself, a steely determination, some might call it wilfulness, surges back to life. She will not be thwarted. It is simply a matter of getting others to agree with her. In cooler moments, in her prayers, she sometimes asks God if her force of will is something she should question; if her capacity to force her will on others is a trait best kept suppressed. But on this matter, she will entertain no doubts. By the time they arrive back at the Rectory, Mildred's supreme confidence, some might say her conviction, has almost convinced Edward that the scheme was his idea in the first place. Now she must persuade William.

## 13

1858 A FEW DAYS LATER

M ildred could bear it no more. She must mend this silly quarrel with Ann. I'll just apologise for asking her to design the window, Mildred decided, even if I don't understand why. Mildred sent a note and took the trap over to the Owen household the next day.

Ann looks sapped, thought Mildred as she bent to kiss the proffered cheek. There were dark rings around Ann's eyes; she seemed bent by the weight of the baby in her arms.

'Let me take Helen!' Mildred's tone was cheery as she stepped inside the house. 'What a picture she is, oh and so heavy now.'

'How good of you to visit.' Ann smiled. 'Do come in, my dear. The girls are longing to see you.'

Neither woman mentioned the row. Perhaps it was the unseasonable heat of the spring day but the girls were noisy and disruptive. The women agreed fresh air was needed. Helen sat up proudly in her perambulator, delightedly grabbing for grasses that waved past her as they ambled down the lane. Lulled by the swaying and dipping of the machine, the baby soon slumped over into sleep. The children's chatter dwindled to desultory disagreements. They found a dry area by a stream and Mildred sat with the girls making daisy chains. Occasional sounds of men at work drifted across from the fields; it was almost soporific. Then Helen woke and started to whimper. Ann stood up wearily. 'I'd better take her back for a feed. Come, girls, home we go.'

As they walked slowly back along the lane, Ann spoke.

'I'm sorry about the other day, Mildred, and I apologise. I'm grateful to you for asking me to make the window, I am. But I am asking you to accept that I cannot do the work. I must turn it down. I have no choice.' Her tone was firm. They walked in silence for a few moments. Then she said: 'So how are the plans for St Mary's going?'

'Oh, well and ... there are developments ... about which I am very excited,' Mildred took a slow breath. 'We've decided to recreate a medieval ceiling.'

'What? A Sistine chapel in Huntingfield?' Ann was intrigued.

'Something like that, I suppose. I'm only an amateur painter but yes, figures, religious motifs, that sort of thing, on the ceiling. And angels, we're going to have angels!'

The baby's carriage jolted to a standstill. Ann's exhaustion dissipated, her expression a mixture of excitement and doubt.

'You? *You* will paint the ceiling?' Mildred nodded.

'But what does William say?'

'That's the part that's proving tricky. William's been difficult about it, he became very angry with me. We were in the church and I was showing him what we've been discussing, Edward and I, the ideas and so on. I told him that I wanted to do it, that *I* would paint the ceiling. William went very quiet and then suddenly he began to raise his voice, shouting. Well, not exactly shouting but very angry! What did I think I was doing? What led me to think I could ... He said it would be too hard for me to do it, too dangerous. The servants heard him shouting. We had a terrible row, Ann, the first really angry words since we were married.'

Ann started to push the perambulator again. Her back was to Mildred. Over her shoulder she tossed the words that fixed in Mildred's mind for the rest of the day.

'You have to see his point. There are those who know that a woman doing that kind of work is simply wrong. Women can do embroidery or paint a picture but they don't paint church ceilings.'

'Ann, this is ridiculous. What do you mean? Why shouldn't I, if I want to?' Mildred hurried after Ann. She wished she could loosen her collar; the atmosphere was stultifying.

'It's not what women do, Mildred. You know that – and you're a vicar's wife as well. It's not setting the right example.'

'William fears that he'll be criticised. What the Bishop will think, what the villagers will say. That's what bothers *him*. But I can't believe it's what *you* think. There's something else, Ann? What is it? Ann, stop and talk to me, please.'

'I don't trust that man,' Ann's low voice was laden with fury. 'Edward Blackburne. There's something about him that I don't … You know he's in love with you. Edward is in love with you, Mildred. He may not know it himself but I do.'

'Be that as it may,' Mildred flared back. 'So is it Edward that you don't like – or me painting the ceiling? It's not clear to me!'

'It's not right,' Ann muttered almost inaudibly, not looking at Mildred.

'Who says?'

Ann shook her head.

'Well this is a shame, a great shame. If you can't support me, then … then we must agree to disagree,' Mildred sounded defiant but she felt devastated. 'I thought I could depend on you, on you of all people Ann. But it seems I cannot.'

Again Ann said nothing.

'Then I must be on my way.' Mildred called out to Sarah and Grace who lingered some distance behind. 'Girls. I've remembered I must be back at the Rectory. I must leave urgently. Escort your mother back to the house, will you?'

And without a backward glance, she set off back to the Owens' house and her trap.

'Who can I rely on?' she shouted as she whipped the horse. 'Come on you fat lazy thing, move yourself!' And as the animal gradually gathered speed and the hedgerows flicked by, her thoughts raced too. First her husband and now her friend, her good friend, did not believe that she could or should paint the ceiling. It was too bad. She must depend on herself now. And, of course, Edward.

Just outside Huntingfield, Mildred guided the trap into a field and tying the horse to a tree walked over to her favourite thinking place. An ancient oak tree, split and twisted but still supporting green growth on one side, it was said that from here the young Queen Elizabeth drew back her bow and with a steady hand shot a deer dead. From childhood, Mildred had admired the monarch for her individuality. The Queen stood firm in the face of opposition from court and the country, ignored those who tried to stand in her way. Mildred would do the same.

As the trap drew up in the Rectory yard, Rose rushed out of the house, her face ashen and a smear on her eyebrow. She'd been blacking the hearth, Mildred thought.

'What's the matter, Rose?' The girl wrenched open the door. 'It's my niece, Ma'am, my sister's girl, Martha. My brother's run up from the village. She's very poorly, a high temper and a red rash on her. Will you help her? That medicine you brought back from your travels. Might it be a cure?'

A year ago Mildred had soothed the impetigo that covered

Rose's arms with an emollient she'd bought in a Moroccan market and it had much improved. For Rose, it became a magical potion. Mildred knew it not would help a feverish child but she could not ignore Rose's pleas.

'I'll get my medicines bag and we'll go to your sister's,' she agreed and within minutes she and the servant took the trap to Mary Fake's cottage.

A stench of sickness. Two children were huddled in one corner while the sick girl lay strewn on a heap of bedclothes in the other. The curtains were closed; the only light flickered from a flame in the grate. But it was enough for Mildred to see a fine rash on Martha's face. Mary, a baby at her breast, was at the girl's side, murmuring softly.

Mildred took a sponge from her medicine bag and began to wipe the girl's red-flecked cheeks, watched her struggle with swallowing. Mildred stripped off the soaked nightgown and saw the rash had spread across the girl's chest and belly and thighs. As she wiped her with cool water, she could feel the tiny bumps on the girl's skin and the heat that rose off her body. Her heart thumped. Mildred had seen symptoms like this before. A blush, which young women find embarrassing and older women crave for its suggestion of youth, is a sign of danger when the skin around the mouth remains pale.

Scarlatina fever. Mildred had nursed another little girl with these symptoms, many years ago. She had sat by another hot bedside throughout a long, bitter night, heard the advice of one doctor who prescribed bloodletting while another advocated ice packs. But nothing had stopped the fine red rash from spreading across that precious body in a gauzy veil of death.

Mildred remained in the cottage for the rest of the night, transfixed, as if by watching each breath, she might save the girl. The eyes of the family followed her every movement, their hopes heavy on her shoulders like a weighty blanket. Her powerlessness was exhausting. At one point, she dropped off to sleep, woke as her head jerked. It was almost dawn and Martha, bright-cheeked, fought for breath. Little snuffles suggested the other children were asleep in a tangled pile. Mildred crept out to the outhouse to relieve herself, almost grateful for the reek of human excrement which stung her wide awake. Mary, blank-faced and withdrawn, paced the floor with her fractious baby, comforting one life as another ebbed away.

Mildred helped Mary to wash her dead daughter before they wrapped the body in cloth for burial. She insisted the family must wash themselves with soap and hot water and the big pot was set to boil the sheets. This would reduce the risk of infection being passed between the family members, she explained. Few village people believed, as Mildred did, in Chadwick's theory of infection. That was fancy London-talk for the rich who had plenty of money for fuel. Village folk believed the fever was due to vapours of 'bad air', miasmas from rotting manure and soil, which caused illness. But Mary was too miserable and exhausted to resist, and did as she was bid.

Mildred walked home. She craved the physical movement, the setting of one foot in front of the other, the ground firm beneath her feet; inside she felt she was falling. Usually she might have gathered bluebells for the table, unable to resist the heavy-scented blooms, but today she could only think of home. The cold bit into her shoulders but she pressed on through the wood, her heart hammering with the effort, and dragged herself up the stairs to her studio.

'William!' The stove was lit and she saw her husband standing in the low warm room, flicking through the drawings laid out along the table. His face was puffy with sleeplessness.

'I've heard the news, my darling wife. It's terrible, poor little Martha is dead. Mary has lost her little girl.'

'It was scarlatina fever, at least I think so,' Mildred sat down wearily.

'Really? Why did you stay, my love, to ...'

'What choice had I? The child was burning away in front of my eyes.' She perched on the sofa, ran her fingers over the soft material. 'Now I fear for the rest of the family, that they might catch the fever. The cottage has been cleaned, the place aired. The father's away, I gather, labouring elsewhere and a message has been sent telling him not to return yet. I sent for the undertaker to remove the body as quickly as possible. The children are terrified of their sister's body lying dead in the corner.'

'They must be. Oh, you've been so brave, Millie. Come lie down here.' William gently coaxed her on to the floor where he'd spread a blanket. He gathered cushions for her head and lay down beside her, wrapped his arms around her.

'I didn't want to do it again, William. Why did the Lord ask it of me?'

'No, never again,' he murmured into her hair. 'My darling girl, rest now after all you've done, and for all that you do ...'

She lingered in the peace of his embrace, felt his warm, dry hand stroke her face, smelt the familiar scent of clean linen on his flesh. He kissed her eyelids, pressing away the dark images of that night and gradually her breathing steadied. She felt safe, touching and touched by things that loved her. And as the horror of the night faded, a surge of desire flooded through her, and the only thing she knew for certain was that she must have him now, here on this makeshift bed; she craved his weight to smother her broken heart and to blot out her terrible memories.

# 14

I t went around the village like wildfire. The Rector was to engage men for renovation work in the church. There was also a rumour that scaffolding was going to be needed, not only for outside repairs but for the *inside.* People were stunned by this news and frantic to find out more. What would the scaffolding be for? One rumour had it that the ceiling was to be painted. Some people found this bizarre, shocking even – those Hollands were madder than snakes – but there were others who were angry that their church was to be changed. We like it the way it's always been, they said, plain and simple. We do not want paintings on the ceilings. Even those who had not been to church for many years agreed.

'And that's my view,' said Judy who would be hard pressed to describe what St Mary's looked like having not been there for over twenty years. 'The Rector is trying to change things and too quickly. I blame his wife.'

Rose was visiting. 'You've heard the talk then? Explains those drawings, doesn't it, the ones I told you about in her studio as she calls it. All those patterns and symbols. And that man, Edward Blackburne, who comes to stay at the Rectory and the three of them, they sit up late, talk and talk. I've heard quarrelling too. The Rector became very angry with her.'

'Really? I heard that she used to paint, before she married the Rector. Perhaps she taking it up again here? But I ask myself, is it with his blessing? I don't agree with it, that's all I know; it's not the sort of work for a married woman. She's a rector's wife and that's her duty, to support him and to bear children. That's enough for any sensible woman. It's in God's hands to bless married people with children. But I sometimes wonder if those who don't fall pregnant, well, they bring it on themselves,' said Judy darkly.

Rose felt disloyal talking about Mildred this way after all that her mistress had done for her family, sitting with Martha when she died, even paying for the funeral. Rose sat biting her lip, trying to stop herself before blurting out a final piece of gossip. 'You know she makes scented infusions,' said Rose. 'I found the teapot one morning, all mucked up in the spout with green foliage. Smelt nice, mind, but I don't know what she used it for. She must have made it in the night.'

'Sounds like mint tea, you ninny,' snipped Judy. 'But you're right. She is a strange woman with very odd behaviour. Poor Mr Holland.'

Sunday services had never been so well attended since rumours about improvements to the church started flying around the village. All that spring, the pews were full each Sunday as people's curiosity drove their feet up the lane, eager to find out more. It was one way to increase congregation sizes, she teased William, create a rumour.

Something associated with Martha's death changed his mind. She was never sure quite what it was. All she knew was that as she had organised the funeral and wake after, their conversations about the church became easier. It was as though William had allowed himself to be persuaded by her. He capitulated and with such charm; she was startled. Now he was her most loyal advocate, telling everyone enthusiastically that she would paint the church. She hoped he was right.

It was summer before they made a public announcement. At the end of the service, just as people were about to make their way out of the church, William stood on the steps of the chancel. He held out his hands: 'One minute please, ladies and gentlemen, if I can have your attention?'

He felt an enormous sense of pride and looked over at Mildred briefly. She barely smiled then lowered her head as he spoke.

'You may have heard rumours of the improvements that we plan for St Mary's. I want to give you all the information that I can so that there is no unnecessary concern about the future of this church, which I have been appointed to care for and which I will protect for as long as I am the Rector here. I am of the conviction, along with many other parsons and our dear Bishop, thinkers in this country and even abroad, that we have allowed our churches to sink into disrepair. That this has not demonstrated our humble respect and faith to God and it has not served you, the congregation, well. It is the duty of the Church to preach the plain truth boldly and it is not God's plan that the poor are oppressed in body or in spirit. It is my view, and one that is shared by many others, including our beloved Bishop, that the church should be a beautiful place wherein we worship together.'

The eyes of the congregation were fixed on William, trying to follow what he was saying. Some looked sceptical while others listened with narrowed eyes but everyone was fixated, keen to hear him out. Only Edward, who stood at the back of the church, looked elsewhere. William followed his gaze; the man had his eyes fixed on Mildred.

He went on: 'Many years ago, our beloved church was desecrated. Like many churches in the area, it fell foul to the puritans who hated beauty, regarding it as heretical and smacking of the Catholic Church. In their zeal, they broke statues, smashed stained glass windows, destroyed murals. I have decided it is my duty, and indeed my joy, to make improvements to St Mary's and to return it to a state of beauty and peace after this mindless destruction. As you know, we have already started. There have been repairs to the roof and the windows which used to leak. We have an altar table here at the east end and, thanks to the kindness of Lady Huntingfield, a stained glass window. It shows the Annunciation and other scenes from the Bible and has been designed and made by a leading London artist.

In addition, you are sitting, comfortably I hope, on pews rather than having to stand for services. I am sure you think this is an improvement! Do notice the carving at the ends – saints, animals and birds – which was done by very skilled local craftsmen from Bungay. Marvellous work. But there will be more. We would like to have embroidered kneelers for all of us to use when we pray. Here is one which has been done by my wife. I hope you agree it's very beautiful. Can I say that any woman who is good at fine needlework might be interested in making one of these splendid kneelers to please come forward and offer her services? Of course there will be payment for this work.'

Mildred saw a few women whispering to each other. She caught Jane's eye but the woman looked away quickly. Then she saw Edward, his head low as though weighed by William's words. Almost immediately he seemed to sense her glance and, peering up under his bushy eyebrows, gave her an imperceptible nod. She remembered Ann's words about Edward's feelings towards her. She looked away.

William continued. 'For the next phase of work, however, we must close our church. From September, there will be no services held here, at least for a time. I hope you will join me in attending the Sunday morning service at Cookley where we have generously been invited to worship. I will lead the walk there from our village.'

There was muttering. It was a longer walk and a big hill to climb up and down to that church and they were unfriendly suspicious folk in Cookley. Few were convinced they'd be welcome, despite what William said.

'Of course, I will still visit the sick and those in need in the village and my cottage lectures will continue, too. Now where was I? Ah yes, the improvements. We will be adding several rooms on to the church, one for the organ, a cloakroom on one side and a vault for the Vanneck family coffins. Next year, you should feel warmer during services. A coke-fed boiler will be installed underneath the church.'

Amazement rustled through the crowd. How much would this cost? Heating that was not an open fire! A few had heard about strange new-fangled ideas of sending warmed air through buildings but wondered how it could work in practice. Still, the Rector was an educated man, committed to progress certainly, and they said he understood science. He had had a water closet fitted at the Rectory, rumour had it, and Thomas didn't have to empty the privy now!

'All these improvements will mean we'll need workmen. I hope some of you will think of coming to work here with us. This will start, probably in September next year. Notices about jobs will be put up in the post office and of course you can speak to me.'

Once harvest was over, there was little casual work available in the area. Renovating St Mary's would bring employment for many men over the winter months, men who would otherwise find it a terrible struggle to feed their families. Bringing good news from the Scriptures satisfied William, but today he was happy to bring news which would fill local bellies.

He looked out across the church. It was quiet, people no doubt stunned by what they'd been told and the scale of the changes talked about. Shafts of coloured light streamed in through the stained glass window and over his shoulder, then danced on the carved edges of the pews. The church was warm today. How beautiful it was already! And here was his faithful flock spread out before him. They had still to hear the final good news. He smiled at Mildred, feeling bountiful and beneficent.

Her face was hidden by her hat. She braced herself for what he was about to say. Her heart beat wildly and her hands, tucked into lace gloves, were moist.

'If you've heard a rumour that the church is going to be painted, I can tell you that it is going to happen. The walls have been whitewashed, as you can see, but what we plan to do will make St Mary's even *more* beautiful. What I would like to announce is that my wife, Mrs Holland, will paint the ceiling herself.'

Who could resist the feeling of power when a crowd of people responds as one? A rumbling gasp bubbled up and then the whole congregation of men, women and children lifted their faces to gaze at the wooden-ribbed ceiling that arched above their heads. Dirty wooden beams, stained plaster, cobwebs and dust were all they saw.

William stood at the door of the church, saying goodbye to the parishioners, shaking hands, asking after ill relatives in the usual way. There was an awkward air to the encounters. A few people made comments about the improvements said how pleased they were to hear something was planned. But others skirted by, awkward, eyes cast down or they mumbled something indistinct. What could they say to the Rector when they thought it was madness? Paint the ceiling? They slipped past if they could, hurrying out so they could talk openly on the walk back to Huntingfield.

Only John Hammant remained. He hobbled forward on crutches. He stood in front of William and held out his hand. 'Thank you for telling us about your plans, Reverend. I want you to know I'm interested, want to be involved and I will watch out for the notices for work, sir.'

'Yes, right, you're interested in the work, John? Very good.' It flashed through William's mind that a man who needs crutches would find it impossible to build, dig and paint.

'Hear me out, Reverend Holland,' said John firmly. Since his accident, the Hammant family had struggled to survive on what Jane and the girls could bring in. No one would employ John now he was 'legless', although, he bitterly joked, they employed men who were legless for other reasons. There were days he wanted to shout out that just because one of his limbs was missing, he was not useless.

'You'll need a gang of men to help you with these repairs. I'm used to working with men, Reverend. I used to do it for the farmer. I ran his threshing team, until the accident, that is. I know the local men that works well and those who are best left at home to tend their vegetables. I may not be able to do the work meself but I am a good organiser of men and you will need that.'

Mildred joined William. 'Morning John,' she said. 'And how is the family?'

John nodded politely. 'Morning Mrs Holland. Very well,

thank you. Jane is outside with the children. I was just explaining to the Reverend. I would like to be part of the gang that works in the church with you, Mrs Holland, and to help in any way I can.'

'Thank you, John. I am going to need it.' Did her smile hide how nervous she felt? She dared not look up to see the wooden beams yawning across the vast space. One person to paint that single-handed? Who had had this ludicrous idea? She had been persuaded by the power of her own words. Now she wondered if she was as mad as they said.

John continued: 'You'll need a team of men, digging, building, bricklaying and so on, and you'll need a foreman to keep the job going. I'm a practical man, sir. Please sir, don't dismiss me.' John fought to control the desperation in his voice. 'You'll need me, sir, to get this work done. And I've got ideas.'

John's eyes were fixed on William's but it was Mildred who answered. 'Come and see me John. I'm ready to listen.'

## 15

Mildred had been a poor student as a girl. Easily bored, she and her sisters had teased the man employed by her father to educate his daughters. They rarely completed the reading, arithmetic or musical practice he set them and pretended to fall asleep in the middle of a lesson or became unaccountably terrified when seeing a spider, clasping at each other, weeping tears of laughter they hoped the teacher mistook for fear. The only lesson that absorbed Mildred was drawing. A less than flattering cartoon of the teacher was found on the classroom floor and thought to be her work. This sketch may have been the final blow to the poor teacher's confidence. Within days he left the family's employment. They later heard he went into trade, selling supplies to gentlemen's milliners.

But now Mildred was a model student. Every piece of information that passed Edward's lips or left his pen was captured and cannibalised with ferocity. The time for talking was done, he had said almost brusquely the last time they met. Ideas were all very well but now they had to work out exactly how they could be executed. She must draft the drawings! Where exactly would she paint? What colours was she proposing to use? How else could he estimate the amounts of materials and tools that would be required and order from the colourman in London? Meantime, he was preparing plans for the other renovations that William wanted; the heating system, and so on. Would she please do the same? Had she not re-read his book on the *fresco secco* method? Well, she must read it again!

She didn't mind his temper at all. She was energised by his exasperation and inspired by his irritation. Each morning a mixture of excitement and dread woke her early. Edward was right; she must put pen to paper and decide what she wanted to create. Some days the ideas flowed like the rain through her pencil on the paper. Other days, doubts dammed the stream.

A little church which she and William had visited in Switzerland was often in her thoughts. They had been travelling along the San Bernardino Pass in Italy some six thousand feet above sea level when William persuaded her to stop for a few days. Reluctantly she had agreed. Not with good grace, however, for her mood was irritable as they hiked over a mountain pass and then down a twisting path to the tiny village of Zillis. It was freezing cold. She could not imagine what they would see here save more impoverished Protestants struggling to survive on the milk their scrawny goats could supply.

William had excitedly pointed to a small church with a tall spiked tower and steep-pitched roof nestling below in the pine trees. 'There it is, Millie, St Martin's!' Exhaustion forgotten, he had hurried over, tripping on a stone. She reluctantly followed, knowing she would only have to climb all the way up the hill again to get back home. The wind ripped at her hat. The wooden door of the church was solid and she could hardly shove it open. Finally, the door yielded and she slipped inside out of the wind. William was engrossed by the ceiling. Looking up, she saw why. Above them stretched panel after square panel of detailed images of saints and men, sea monsters and fishtailed creatures, dragons and sirens, bordered with intricate and coloured patterns. William said: 'Marvellous, don't you think? Over one hundred panels, each with its own story. The ones in the centre, can you see? Stories from the life of Jesus, the flight into Egypt, the crowning with thorns, carrying the cross and one of him healing the moonstruck boy, the boy with epilepsy ... and from the life of St Martin. The church is dedicated to him.'

'It's astounding. Who did the painting?'

'Perhaps a Roman? There's evidence of Roman settlement and graves here from the sixth century. Others think the painting was done a bit later. It became known in the 1470s when the Viamala road we took yesterday across the Alps was first opened up as a trade route to Italy and the coast.'

They sat where they could prop their heads comfortably and study the ceiling. It was a relief to be out of the wind but the church was still bitterly cold.

'What kind of person would consider doing something so difficult?' Mildred shook her head. 'The painter would never have imagined that all these years later, his work would still exist and be admired.'

'Perhaps it was a woman who was the painter! A persistent woman like you, my love.' William had kissed her hand, and then they had started back, keen not to be out on the mountainside in the dark.

Subsequently, she had often thought about that lonely church. Who was the person who had laboured in that cold and poorly-lit place, day after day? What kind of person could be fixated on such a vast, intricate and painstaking task in the sure expectation that few outside his village would ever see it? Only God would be his witness. Now she asked herself: was she embarking on a similar road?

It was the wettest autumn that anyone could remember. Every day the rain poured down until the fallow fields became lakes and the stream that ran through the village flooded cottages clustered on its bank. William had gone with a team of men to clear away the muddy aftermath. Rose had been instructed to gather dry clothes and food for the temporarily homeless families. But William insisted Mildred must stay to meet John Hammant. She must not be deflected from her work.

There was a cold drizzle and she was pleased not to be trudging across the yard to spend another day in the studio. She felt unsettled and nervy. She pushed inside the church. The cold circled her neck like a coil. Despite the white walls, the church interior was gloomy. There was John, staring up at the stained glass window, hunched over his crutches, one trouser leg neatly tucked up at the back. He wheeled round as he heard her enter and made his way slowly towards her. It flashed through her mind that he was more incapacitated than she remembered.

'Good morning, John. Thank you for coming up to the church. It seemed the most logical place to meet. Will you sit?' He manoeuvred himself on to a pew seat on one side of the aisle while she sat on the other. They both looked up at the ceiling. Neither spoke and the longer there was silence, the harder it seemed to break. In an odd way, she found it relaxing. Then they both started speaking at once.

'I am able to help you, Mrs ...'

'I'm not sure John how you can help ...'

It struck her as ludicrous, to be sitting almost in the dark with a man she barely knew, a cripple, about to talk about painting a rough surface that was over fifty feet up in the air. She gave a low guffaw and he, misunderstanding her humour, said desperately: 'Don't doubt me, Mrs Holland, please.'

She understood at once. 'I don't doubt you John. I wasn't laughing at you at all but at myself. Please, go on.'

He spoke tentatively. 'I want to help you with this work and I can do it. When you're painting, there needs to be someone to organise the men doing the new building and the repair work. There's a lot that will be going on in the church and, while you're busy up there painting the ceiling, you'll need someone down here directing the men to do the rest.'

'Go on,' she said.

John nodded: 'I will be your foreman. I'll organise the men under your direction. I used to do it for the farmer. I was good at it then and I'll be good at now, Mrs Holland. I know the men around here. I know who is good at their work, who needs a bit of watching. The Reverend and you – you can rely on me.'

Desperation had scarred his face. The pain of the last two years, losing his mobility and his ability to feed his family, watching his wife struggle home with the meagre coins of poor relief jingling in her pocket, it must be dreadful. Mildred knew their eldest daughter had left school to take a maid's position on the Beccles estate so there was one less mouth to feed.

'If I need to get about, I have me crutches and me wheeled chair. I do it round about home and I can do it here. And I can read and write, did you know that?' There was pride in his voice as John continued: 'I'll keep notes of the materials used, check off deliveries, list up what we need ... I can manage it, Mrs Holland. You must believe me.'

It was clear the man had carefully considered the practicalities of what she'd need. Mildred, obsessed by what and how she would paint, hadn't considered how she'd manage the rest of it. The man had a point. Having a foreman would leave her to paint in peace. Previously overwhelmed by the scale of the task, now she saw she need not work unaided. When Mildred held out her hand, she saw it was trembling.

'Thank you, John. Yes, what you suggest is a marvellous idea.

Will you help me to make St Mary's beautiful again – will you? We start next September.'

Christmas had come and gone, and beyond a polite exchange of cards, she had not heard from Ann. Mildred sent the occasional letter; last summer she'd suggested taking the children to the beach at Walberswick, in the autumn she had asked them to the bonfire on Guy Fawkes Night and in January, when the pond froze over, to come skating. But Ann had refused these invitations, politely enough, but there was no suggestion the women should meet again.

Mildred was miserable. Most days she talked to Ann in her head, challenging her, asking her how she could be so stubborn. Mildred had always sensed there was something unpredictable about Ann, something secretive and elusive. Was she trustworthy? Mildred had hoped she and Ann were becoming true friends but now she fretted she had lost her friend, perhaps for good. When William asked why the women didn't visit anymore, Mildred made an excuse about being too busy with work.

At the start of the year, the weather remained squally and wet. Even the oak trees looked forlorn and soaked in the drizzle. Rose gazed out of the window across the pale green fields. Mr Blackburne was expected that afternoon. He had not visited in several weeks. Rose wondered if the church project had been abandoned.

It was still raining hard when the bedraggled architect rode into the Rectory yard. Thomas took his horse, and Edward hurried over to the studio, Rose quickly following with hot refreshments and a towel. As the girl climbed the short flight of steps into the studio, she felt the heat of the animals stabled beneath warming the air. Putting the tray down on a side table, she noticed her mistress was shivering despite being wrapped in a woollen shawl. Edward stood at the far end of the room. Rainwater pooled at his feet.

'Rose, good, please give Mr Blackburne some tea.' Her mistress turned towards the architect. 'I'm sure you understand, Edward, I feel somewhat hesitant to show you my drawings. But, as you say, we cannot proceed without them.'

Mildred flung the shawl on the floor and, her arms now free, lifted a ream of paper on to one end of a long table. 'You may feel they are too grand, Edward, perhaps too simple or not appropriate. I don't know. There's no way round this, come and have a look! Rose, come here, hold this edge.'

Rose wasn't sure exactly what Mildred wanted her to do. The girl moved uncertainly towards the table and flinched as Mildred took her arm, dragged her to the table and pressed her fingers firmly on to a large roll of paper.

'Use your other hand to hold the corner, Rose. Firm now, while I unroll it!' Rose watched in amazement as her mistress unfurled the ream of paper to reveal a huge drawing. It looked like a person who was kneeling. It wore a crown. 'Come closer, Edward. Why, you'll not be able to see what I have done from over there.'

'I'm wet from the rain, Mildred.'

'Yes of course, I am sorry, I should have thought. Rose, fetch that towel will you? No, wait! I need you to hold the paper down. Oh fiddle. It's not a problem, Edward, it's only a draft. Come over here and drip as much as you like. What I need to know is... What do you think?'

Rain from Edward's coat plopped on to an almost life-sized form of a kneeling angel. The figure, draped in folds, had huge stretched wings and held a scroll in its hands. 'Have you any others?' he asked.

Rose helped Mildred to unfurl another roll of paper. This revealed another drawing; an angel with a cross. All in all, there were twelve rolls of paper, each one showing a winged and kneeling figure clasping a different emblem of the Passion. Then a final drawing of a pelican pecking at its breast and feeding its young on the blood that dripped from the wound.

'These figures would be for the highest parts of the ceiling,' Mildred explained. 'I've counted the number of roof beams and there is a space between each one for an angel as well as a panel for the pelicans. That would mean the whole ceiling over the chancel is covered.'

Her mistress looked anxiously at the architect, for the man had not spoken for some time. Hands clasped behind his back, the only sound that could be heard was the plop of rain falling from his beard on to paper. Mildred turned up the flame of a second lamp. She grabbed the shawl again, flung it around her shoulders and paced restlessly around the studio.

'I've other ideas for the lower parts of the ceiling, where it meets the wall. And I'll decorate the architrave too. Let me show you.' She fetched another sheaf of drawings. 'Hold this, Rose, hold it flat. You can see, Edward, designs for the Lamb of God for one part, the keys of Heaven for another part. Monograms for the Vanneck family and one for our family. And these ... patterns for the borders and so on, the colours I want ...'

Still Edward was silent. He continued to leaf through the drawings haphazardly scattered along the table. The pitch of Mildred's voice rose again. 'Have you nothing to say, Edward, nothing at all? What do you think of it all?'

Rose drew herself back as far as she could against the wall, no longer acting as a stop to paper curling; several rolls slipped on to the floor. Her mistress was becoming distressed by the architect's strange silence. If only Rose could slip away. She longed to be back in the house, sweeping the pantry or dusting the parlour. She had seen Mildred get upset before and dreaded seeing it again; the tear-streaked face, the abandoned sobbing.

'I've designed patterns for the roof beams, plotted colour schemes for the carved angels. I've done so much but you won't ...' Arms flung out, Mildred wildly indicated a pile of drawings on a nearby chair. 'Edward. Why won't you say anything? Do you not like the work?' Mildred was visibly upset now, her breath coming in short bursts, her lips trembling.

The man looked up as if woken from a dream. Rose saw his hair was damp, his collar stained from where the rain had run down his face. His eyes were heavy-lidded, his mouth loose.

'How can you doubt it?' Suddenly he burst out and arms outstretched, strode over to Mildred and took hold of her hands. Gazing into her face, he cried: 'It's wonderful work, Mildred! I just didn't expect it, that's all. I hoped but I didn't know if ... if you were talented!'

Almost as quickly, he moved away from her to rifle through the drawings. As though it had been his presence which had held her upright, Mildred collapsed into a chair and buried her face in the shawl. There was a pause, then: 'Are you sure?' she whispered.

'I am sure,' Edward replied. He raised his voice. 'Mildred! Look at me. I am sure.'

Rose saw her mistress raise her head and look, as directed, at the architect. For what seemed an age, the studio was still. Rose wanted to slip away; she felt uncomfortable as though she was seeing something private. Finally, Edward spoke. 'I hope you're not frightened of heights?'

'No,' Mildred replied, dipping her head. Rose wondered how she knew her mistress was lying.

It was a recurring dream. Mildred stood on the scaffolding in the church. But each time she dipped her brush into the paint and raised it to the ceiling, the colour slid off the bristles and formed coloured balloons which floated away. The dream often woke her. William stroked her shoulder, said she was bound to feel anxious about starting this big piece of painting.

In the daytime, the sight of John directing men to unload a cart piled high with materials, tools and equipment into the yard sheds made her feel nervous.

'But I have every confidence in you, my darling,' said her husband kissing her hand with an exaggerated bow. 'The church will look splendid and we will have to turn away the hordes of people who will want to admire and worship our beautiful church!'

She wanted gold; of that she was clear. In a letter she asked Edward to bring samples. Days later the architect arrived, handed her a parcel and then began to flick through the recent sketches she'd been working on. She felt a flash of annoyance; why does he assume he can look at my work without asking? The parcel was heavy, much weightier than she expected. The brown paper wrapping was stamped with the name Cornelissen, the most romantic of names it seemed to her. Inside were five small books, each one containing paper-thin gold sheets separated by tissue paper. Champagne, red, lemon, white, green. It had never occurred to her that gold had so many hues.

'You can use gold paint on the lettering.' Edward pointed to a monogram she fashioned from the letters IHC, the abbreviation of the Latin Holy name for Jesus. 'But to highlight the angel's halos or wings, it will be better to use gold leaf. You must choose the colour of gold that you like best.'

The gold sheets shimmered under her fingers. 'They're all exquisite, Edward. How can I!'

He began to explain to her how the leaf was applied. In his usual tedious way, she thought, so complex and detailed. 'The area to be gilded must be clean from dust and dirt. And then prepared by using a gold "size" or sticky substance which, after several hours will set until it's just tacky enough to ...'

Her mind wandered. She imagined that she was applying the gold to the tip of an angel's wing ... and it glittered as the light caught its rich surface ...

Edward droned on: '... and then finally, a layer of animal skin glue which will act as a seal to protect the gold from damage. Work out how much will be needed and I will place an order. Mildred?' Edward looked at her. 'You've not been listening, have you? Read up on it in one of the books I brought and practise here before you start in the church.'

'Yes, of course. Now we should go to the Rectory. I've been here all day and William will be back soon. He'll want to see you.'

'But before we do, I just wanted to say ...' Edward moved closer and took Mildred's hand between his own. 'I admire you, Mildred, for your persistence and the courage you show, for what you're about to do.'

It was like a bee had stung her; she snatched her hand away. 'Edward, please!'

And stepping away from him, she escaped down the stairs, the leaves of gold fluttering in her wake.

# 16

M ildred knocked firmly and peered in at the door of the tailor's shop.

'Good morning, Mr Edwards. I'm Mrs Holland from the Rectory.'

Mr Edwards, the tailor, was sitting at a long table, sewing a piece of cloth. He looked up slowly, as though he had heard a noise he couldn't quite place. For a moment he stared at the woman who stood in the door of his shop. He had never had a visit from the Rector or his wife in all the years he'd had a business. Most of his customers where farmhands, a young lad getting married and needing a suit or a local woman after a piece of lace to decorate the sleeve of a dress.

Tom to his immediate family, but Mr Edwards to everyone else, stood up and looked down. The garment on his lap slipped to the floor. It was gloomy in the shop except for a pool of light from the gas lamp. Someone looking closely would have seen his hand shaking. Uncertain and awkward, a tall man with a stoop, he addressed the floor: 'Mrs Holland, a pleasure.'

Mildred stepped inside the shop. There was a particular smell; she couldn't quite place it, of new cloth perhaps mingled with gas and sweat. Rolls of material were stacked along one side of the room and there were boxes and a few hats in a tumbled stack by the window. She could make out a rack of ribbons in one corner and buttons on a tray, things for women, but she wondered how recently another female had been there. The place said 'man'; where a person might stand only once in his lifetime and be fitted for the suit in which he would be married and buried.

She set her bag on the floor and pulled off her hat. 'I need a pair of trousers, Mr Edwards. For myself.'

The tailor didn't reply. He was standing some distance from her but even in the low light she could see embarrassment spread like a stain up his neck. The man shifted on his feet and rubbed his jaw.

'A pair that a man would use for working. That will suit me.' Her voice was firm. She'd heard that women convicts, facing the rope, asked to wear trousers to protect their dignity from the leering crowds which gathered round the gallows. Crowds would gather close up to where the victim would hang to see what was revealed when the death kicks started. For her, high on the scaffolding, trousers would provide warmth as well as modesty.

'Mr Edwards. Can you help me? Fit me with a pair that will be suitable?'

The tailor cleared away pieces of material from a chair, gestured for her to sit down and then disappeared through a door. Mildred sat in the semi-gloom knowing that gossip and tittle-tattle would be round the village in a few days; Mrs Holland was to wear man's clothes. And even though William said he didn't mind what the village thought, he must wish sometimes she did not want to do these odd things. Mildred straightened her hat.

Mrs Edwards appeared. She was as short as her husband

was tall. Were her eyes wide with alarm or distaste? Mildred wondered.

'You've come for some trousers.' Mrs Edwards said. The words were spit out like sour fruit. Her face was stony and, with an upward nod of the head, she indicated that Mildred should stand. She stretched up to circle Mildred's waist with a tape measure. Mildred saw the pink scalp, the tiny pieces of dandruff that clung to odd hairs, and felt Mrs Edwards' large warm breasts as they briefly pressed against her legs. The whiff of sweat and talc. Mildred held herself stiff and unbending. Drawing back to read the tape, Mrs Edwards' eyes lifted briefly to meet Mildred's; they contained not a flicker of understanding.

'What is so wrong with what I am doing?' Mildred wanted to shout. But she remained silent, burning inside, as the rest of her measurements were taken, listened as these were called out to the tailor who was, Mildred assumed, presumably hiding in the back room.

Then Mrs Edwards bustled off to join him. Mildred stood in the gloom. 'I will be painting the church ceiling,' Mildred called out to no one in particular. 'I need these trousers so I can work and be warm. Please will one of you show me some thick material, the best for the job?'

After some time, Mr Edwards reappeared. He had a length of brown wool material in his arms. Head down, he held it out to Mildred who pretended to examine it. But humiliation made her eyes sting. She dropped to the chair.

'We've heard your plan,' said Mrs Edwards gruffly and stood close to where Mildred sat. No taller than Mildred's shoulder, she blazed bitterness. 'But why would you do it?' It was a question that expected and would receive no answer. It hung on the air like a dead weight.

'Be ready in a week's time,' Mr Edwards folded the material

and looked straight into her eyes. Mildred looked back at him, proud and stiff.

'Because it will be beautiful, and the church will be full of colour, and there will be angels, and ...' She could think of nothing else to add, rather there were no words in a hundred dictionaries which could supply the answer.

# 17

William stirred early. Mildred was already awake. Sweat lay like a limp cloth around her body. 'Shall we pray together?' she whispered, and they slipped from the bed to kneel. Her forehead pressed to the blankets, their smell and warmth and the sound of her husband's murmured incantations comforted her. 'Keep her safe,' she heard him say and was grateful for his supplication.

'I'll fetch the tea,' he said, clambering to his feet. 'I can hear Cook in the kitchen, Rose won't be about yet.'

William left her in the early morning gloom. She could not look at the mound of material that slumped over a chair in an exhausted heap: her painting clothes. It would be easy to change her mind if she did so now, stop all this nonsense; it was not too late. She would tell William she had changed her mind and he would understand, and she could lie back against the pillows and plan a quiet day. It was the trousers that unnerved her the most. Those headless legs which straddled the chair with bravado. Were they laughing at her, daring her to use them?

She sidled over and reached instead for the long johns, pale worms curled on the floor. She remembered her father wore them under his working clothes and, to the irritation of his wife, sat by the fire in them in the evening 'warming his bones'. He would pull Mildred on to his lap and gently scratch her head, which she loved, and tell her of his day on the farm. If her father could see her now, what would he think?

She held the long johns out at arm's length; they dangled limp and powerless. Daring to poke one foot in at the top, she drove her leg down the cotton tunnel of the legging, feeling the dry grip of the material; now the other leg. Then the tweed trousers, rough to the touch, pulled up and fastened with a button round her waist. More comfortable than stays, she thought, I'd never have known. A vest was drawn over her head to lie close over her breasts and belly, then a shirt and finally a long smock which draped almost to her knees. Men's boots fastened with buttons on the side to protect her feet. She stood at the mirror, twisting her hair up into a knot.

William appeared in the doorway with the tea.

'Well ... and what are you smiling at?' She wanted to be angry with him but there was no denying she looked bizarre. They both laughed.

'You look wonderful, my darling,' he bent to circle his arms around her, 'like a beautiful boy!'

'No, your deluded forty-four-year-old wife. Who must eat her breakfast and get to work!' And she shook him off and swept out of the room.

Approaching the church, her confidence drained away again. Heading into the churchyard was like wading through mud, each step an act of sheer will. Past the yew tree, around the headstones, along the path and there was the church, the place where she had, for so many years, sought solace. Now it seemed a place of dread.

She pushed at the heavy door, arms weak with anxiety, and stepped into the milky interior, frowning at the sight of the scaffolding, the spindly wooden structure that crouched like an enormous spider and would pin her to the ceiling like a fly in its web.

'I could not climb that ladder,' William's words echoed in her head.

Some weeks earlier, a brown parcel had arrived at the Rectory. Inside it a pair of fingerless gloves, crocheted in thin grey silk, and a piece of card:

*Dearest Mildred, I hope these will keep your fingers nimble and lively as you paint. I will think of you over these next months and hope to come and see your splendid work one day. With love, Elizabeth*

Mildred dug into her pockets and drew on the gloves. They lay smooth against her skin. Then her fingers reached out for the ladder and she started to climb. All was going well until the seventh rung when her legs suddenly refused to obey. She asked her leg to raise her foot to the next rung; it did not do what she requested. At the same time, her knees took on a life of their own. They began to shiver, the skin over the joint quivering like a blancmange. Panic fizzed in her chest. Her heart thumped. Cold air swirled around her ankles. She sensed the open space around her neck and her head. She gulped and wondered if she would ever move again. Except for her trembling knees, she had frozen.

Her mind raced. She had to climb the ladder if she wanted to paint. But then that voice, the one which reminded her that she could always change her mind, started up again. No one could expect her to do this Herculean task. She could simply descend the ladder, and put her feet back on solid ground. The church would remain as it was, like many other churches in this very county, without a medieval painted ceiling. God would understand. He knew of her terror of heights and how difficult it would be to spend the next – who knew how long – suspended some fifty feet above the world. She was not a painter. She was the wife of the Rector of Huntingfield!

Through this cacophony of thought, she became aware of a sound. Not William who was murmuring encouragements from the base of the ladder. No, another that she couldn't quite place. It was her! Her gasps for breath, short rasps of air which stung her throat with needles of cold. She began to feel dizzy, her fingers and lips to tingle and then there was the sensation of water streaming into her mouth. I am going to be sick, she thought. I must not look down.

But her eyes immediately disobeyed, swivelling down to the sea of upturned faces that swirled beneath her. Round eyes, round mouths gazing up in disbelief. Everyone in the church was watching. William's mouth was moving, workmen were scratching their heads, John sat in his chair, pale with concern Rose clung to a pew, her face frozen in incredulity. Only Edward seemed nonchalant, standing to one side with arms folded, regarding her with calm equanimity. He looked at her almost dispassionately, his eyes locked on hers. And then he nodded, slowly, deliberately.

She dragged her eyes forward and fixed them. Now her mouth was powder dry and her heart banged in her chest. She forced her hands up the side of the ladder, the silk of the gloves sliding over the smooth wood, until her arms were stretched above her head. She commanded her left leg to bend and to move upwards. Bizarrely, and for no reason she could understand, the leg obeyed her and it travelled, settling on the rung above. She felt a frisson of hope. Gripping the sides of the ladder as hard as she dared, she commanded her knee to straighten and she felt the power of her muscles as she rose up through the cold air, the bones taking her weight. She had moved up a rung.

Keeping her eyes forward, she commanded her hands to slide up again and now her fingers to stop and grip while her right foot set off on its blind, uncertain journey to find a higher secure place, an anchor point where it could settle and fix. Then the command again for her muscles to contract and up she soared, up, up into the air.

And in this steady way, Mildred climbed and as she did, a sense of triumph lifted her; and though the flimsy frame dipped and danced with her shifting weight, she rose as though climbing to heaven.

# 18

Mildred had reached the highest scaffolding platform only feet from the church ceiling. But she could not stand, not to start with. Stepping on to the wooden platform, she had dropped to her knees with terror and relief. It had taken several minutes for the waves of nausea to subside. A memory of when she was quite young, two or three perhaps, came into her mind. Her father was lifting her, screaming, on to his horse and settling her on the saddle in front of him. His arms were wrapped around her waist and he whispered into her hair, describing all that could be seen from so high up. And she had stopped wailing and rested back against her father's chest, felt the comfort of his rumbling voice through his solid frame, saw through her tears the things he pointed out to her, and was secure.

'Take my elbow,' she directed the workman who was waiting there. Like a young foal finding its legs for the first time, she stood up. Now feeling braver, she reached for the massive rough-grained beam which ran the length of the building. The spine of a beast, from its curved ribs hung the walls. She half-listened for its breath.

She dared to look around the platform. There was her painting box. Only this morning, she had checked again that her pencils and paints and brushes were in place. Her bag of drawings, tools, paints, turpentine and palette had all been winched up the scaffold and were piled on one side.

'You can leave now,' she commanded, for she now was in control.

Her shoes tapped on the boards as she laid out her temporary studio. Pots and boxes in the middle, tools at one end and the cushions and blanket strewn against the wall to make a comfy resting place. Only the top of the altar window poked up above the level of the scaffold floor but it gave some light.

Panels had been fixed between each rafter. On these pale surfaces she must paint the images which had gestated for so long in her mind. With a mixture of triumph and trepidation, she dragged over a stool and stood on it to examine where she would begin.

She had worried too that the thought that only thin wooden boards prevented her from plunging to the floor beneath would distract her from work. But once she began, the only thing in her mind was painting.

First, she took a piece of tracing paper on which she had already drawn an image, and fastened it to the panel with little tacks. Having taken the correct measurements, the paper fit the area perfectly. Using a needle, she pricked around the main shapes of the design: a kneeling angel, a crown and wings, leaving a tiny trail of holes. A soft brush dipped in coal dust was then patted along the dots, puffing dust through the holes. Holding her breath in trepidation, she lifted the tracing paper away. She beamed to see what lingered there; the ghostly shape of her first angel.

In pencil, she sketched in the finer details of the face, the curls of the hair and the feathers of the wings. She outlined areas where colour and shading defined contour and shape. Squatting back on her heels, she surveyed the completed drawing. Painting could start.

She had just set out the brushes and pots of pigments when the scaffold started to shudder. It took her moments to realise this meant someone was coming up the ladder. Who was to disturb her peace? Edward's head appeared at the scaffold's edge and then he climbed the final rungs. Brushing the dust carefully off his suit, he handed her a flagon.

'Good morning, Mildred. I thought I'd come to see how you were getting on.'

She opened the flask. The smell of hot beef tea was delicious and she realised how hungry she was.

Edward was inspecting what she had done so far; touchiness jagged through her. 'It's going well,' he said quietly. 'How are you coping?'

'I'm fine, thank you. Yes, I am able to work.' She sipped the tea.

'Not started painting yet? I'm interested to see the quality now paint's provided in these collapsible tubes.'

'I'm about to start. And I've got linseed oil if I need to thin it.'

Reluctant to engage in conversation, she peered down over the edge of the scaffolding. Other work was going on below: John and one of the workmen were constructing a wooden structure, she was not sure of its purpose. How strange it was to spend the day seeing people only from a great height, their pale figures indistinct in the gloom. As her darling angels would come to see the world.

'I must start again, Edward.' She knelt down over her paint box, hoping he would take the hint.

'I'll stay for a while to watch if that's acceptable?' It was not, she thought, but gave a curt nod.

The surface of each panel had been prepared a few days

previously by a workman, slightly roughened with sanding paper so the pigments would fix to the 'key'. Having already painted a smaller version of the angel in her stable studio, she knew where and which colours were needed. She worked fast; the plaster surface drank the pigment greedily. She squeezed out only small amounts of paint from the metal tubes so that it did not spoil in the cold conditions.

Edward stood at her shoulder. 'It's taking well.'

She barely heard him, just shook her head. She applied the main blocks of colour: cream for the robe, yellow for the hair, pale brown for the wings, an iridescent blue for sky. It was tiring to work with arms outstretched and her head bent back but she pressed on for it was only when she could add the shading and detail that she would have a sense of how the whole schema would look. Now she began on the details of the face, fingers and nails, strands of hair, the fastening on the kneeling angel's robe.

It was now late afternoon; most of the daylight had gone and the candles could not provide sufficient light. She suddenly realised how much she ached and crouched down to relieve the pain in her back. She was panting.

'Mildred, you must finish now. The light is too poor for you to work properly,' Edward urged. She'd almost forgotten he was still there.

'I know. Just leave me for a few moments, I'd be grateful.'

'Anything I can take down for you?'

'Only this. I'll be down shortly.'

Now she was alone with her angel. Its face was indistinct, still emerging from the paint, but already she loved it. It seemed a ridiculous thing to do but do it she must. She kissed her fingers and planted them on the lips of her beautiful creation.

Going down the ladder was almost as frightening to her as climbing up it had been. For she had to lower herself while her foot blindly searched for the rung beneath. Ah, the sense of relief when it found its place of safety.

'Twenty rungs!' the workman counted her down from where he stood below with a lighted lamp.

My angel watches over me, she told herself, and glanced up quickly to see the faint face looking down at her. Two more ladders to descend and she was back on terra firma. Daylight had disappeared; she could barely make out where she had spent all day, so dark was it up there. The first day was over. How many more to go?

## 19

Sore cracked fingers woke her. A brief moment of peace and then she remembered that here again was another day to spend staring up at a ceiling only inches away from her face. A squeeze of anxiety seeped along her veins and creeping fingers twisted her belly. She rolled out of bed and squatted over the chamber pot, breathing in the warm scent of urine.

'Your hair smells of paint.' William kissed her softly on the top of her head. 'And you didn't wash carefully enough. There are spots of paint on your face.' He smiled at her. 'My clever wife.'

'I'm full of aches and pains.'

'But you're so brave. Edward says so. Up there, so high. You're not frightened?'

'No,' she lied.

'So how is the ruination of St Mary's?' Judy said. 'Close the window, will you, there's a terrible draught.'

It was a warm day for autumn so Rose reluctantly did as she

was asked. Best not to infuriate Judy, not if you wanted to ask her something.

'Well, it was touch and go on the first day that she made it up the ladder at all. Thought she was going to fall. She don't like heights. But now, end of the first week, she seems to manage all right.'

'You go and watch? What about your work?'

'She gets me to fetch the draft drawings from her studio.' There was more than a hint of pride in Rose's voice.

'What do you mean, draft drawings?' said Judy. 'And you *take* them to her, up on that tall scaffold?'

Judy was interested. Rose happily pulled a chair up to the bedside.

'Yes, she's already drawn them on big bits of paper, big rolls, up there in the studio. Did that some time ago, of course. Showed them all to that Mr Blackburne from London. Made her nervous, it did.'

'The drawings, Rose, you take them to her?' Judy said impatiently.

'I fetch'em for one of the men to take up. When she starts a new figure.'

'What do you mean – figure?'

'Angels, you know, she's drawing angels across the ceiling with big wings. And they'll be painted in gold. Real gold.'

The women looked at each other, shaking their heads in disbelief.

'But there's stranger goings on up there at the Rectory, Judy.'

'Stranger than plastering our church in real gold? And what might that be?'

'On the second day of the painting. Mrs Holland found it, fixed to the door of the porch. A coil of rowan.'

'You don't say. Really?'

The women exchanged looks.

'And on the Friday morning, right by the door of the church, she saw the soil had been disturbed. She got John to have a look, and he dug up a bottle, stopped tight, filled with nails and brown liquid. Got Walton to smash it. Vinegar inside.'

Judy inhaled sharply.

'What do you say to that, Judy? Do you know what that means?'

'It's obvious, isn't it? Some call it a witch's bottle. It's put it under a doorway to frighten off spirits and such like. Someone's trying to tell her they don't like what she's doing.'

Rose looked dubiously.

Judy said. 'There's plenty 'round here who's not happy with what's going on.'

'Witchcraft? Lord, that's not right, Judy.'

'Does the Rector know?'

'Don't think so. When John found the bottle, Mrs Holland told 'im not to tell a soul, to keep it a secret. I only knows 'cos Owen Walton told me, and he swore me not to tell anyone. Oh, goodness, now I've told you. You won't mention to anyone, will you, Judy?'

'Course not,' said Judy soothingly. 'You know me. I never gossip.'

She couldn't admit to William that when she woke each morning, there was only a moment of quiet before her doubts started. Whatever made her take on this momentous task? It was going to take her months. Last week there were two afternoons when she had to scrub off most of what she had painted that morning. She had almost cried with fury and spent the evening choked by anger or exhaustion, she wasn't sure which. And now these silly items that had been left about the church. John had looked incensed when that bottle full of bent nails was dug up. Country spells, he'd told her shaking his head, old-fashioned ways that were best ignored. She found it amusing to think of some deluded villager dreaming up ways to frighten her. Amusing but if she was honest, a little unsettling, too. But he or she, whoever it was, wouldn't succeed. Mildred was not going to be distracted by superstition and ignorance. Still, it was better not to tell William; he'd only worry. She didn't want to give her husband any more reasons to be concerned.

So that Sunday when she had walked with William to Cookley church for the service, she buckled on an invisible coat, one that was strong enough to bat off what she supposed were the sneers of the villagers. But also, she hoped, shielded her from the spite of whoever was trying to frighten her. Was that person there on the walk to Cookley, worshipping, singing, kneeling to pray?

It was when she was working high up on the scaffolding, alone except for her angels and her thoughts, that she sometimes felt perturbed. If someone was creeping around the church, what else might they get up to? How she would love to have discussed it all with Ann. She would find it exasperating or entertaining, probably both. How much she missed her dear friend!

So it was with her sister that Mildred shared her qualms.

*Dear Elizabeth*

*I was glad to hear that the move is complete and that Father and Mother have started to settle into the new house. Lincoln is a more practical place for you all to live than the farm house was, and though you will have only one maid living in, being in town will mean you can hire additional help as and when it is needed. I am sure Mother's confusion will clear when she settles into a routine. Do speak to the doctor about a sleeping draught if she continues to wander at night.*

*I am so busy with the painting and in little need of entertainment in the evenings. Spending the day up on the scaffolding leaves me interested only in the warmth of the fire. It can be very chilly! But let me entertain you with a strange Suffolk tale. Someone, it seems, is unhappy with my work in the church. He or she, I don't know who, is leaving little signs for me; spells which are thought to ward off evil. I'm ignoring them, of course, but have decided not to tell William. I don't want to give him any excuse to stop me and you know how he worries. So I press on and hope that the painting and building will all be complete so that the church is open in time for Easter. Know that I think of you each day when I put on the gloves you made for me!*

*Best wishes to you all, Mildred*

A daily rhythm developed. Mildred arrived at the church just after dawn and as the light crept in through the windows, watched her angels awake. As the ceiling of St Mary's filled with figures, she felt the happiness not only of progress but of creation. A physical experience of satisfaction, of literally being filled up.

How unlikely, absurd even, that the simple act of applying pencil to plaster could create this feeling of contentment. The anxiety and dislocation which had sometimes threatened to overwhelm her in the past had become absorbed in the routine activity of working. Despite the cold and the dark and her vertigo, as the shapes formed and the colours sang, she felt released from the uncertainty which had lived with her for so long.

John arrived soon after eight. Within days she realised how much she depended on this methodical man. He worked from his wheeled chair when he needed to use his hands or with other tasks on his crutches. His careful ways, organisation and air of authority gave her confidence and courage. Once they had discussed the plans for the day and agreed what needed to be done, her materials were winched up the scaffolding. She could then forget the hive of activity going on below her; John was in charge.

There were personal daily battles to fight; her vertigo, for example. She learnt the trick about climbing up. As long as she looked straight ahead, she could convince her shaking knees to bend and straighten, to lever up her weight, to move up the ladder. Her heart might thump, her stomach lurch and her arms shake but she fixed her eyes and focused on taking methodical steps.

But coming down the ladder still terrified her. Not knowing precisely where to place her foot on the rung beneath but being unable to look down for fear of overwhelming nausea was frightening. If it was bitterly cold, she might have to make the trip several times a day so she could warm up by the brazier. There was a danger in letting her hands and feet get too cold for she might not be able to get herself down to the ground in the evening. Otherwise she worked on until the light failed and the lamps that hung around her like so many stars could not illuminate the walls.

Not since she was a child had she sat been able to sit on the floor cross-legged, fearing to compromise her modesty. Now, liberated by her trousers, she happily sat in this comfortable position when painting the lower wall areas. Otherwise she stood and, for those panels nearest to the ceiling, she used a ladder, one hand supporting the weight of her head while the other stretched out above her head to work. Sometimes both arms went numb. All in all, the process was exhausting.

Nevertheless, as each week passed, she became stronger and fitter and could work more efficiently. Familiarity with the techniques meant she made fewer mistakes and learnt clever shortcuts and tricks. And as her skills increased, so did her enjoyment. Only the strange 'signs' threatened to spoil her cheerful mood. It was easy enough to deal with the sprigs of meadowsweet she found strewn across the church entrance. They made a pretty arrangement stuck in a jar on the church windowsill. But the curious arrangement of birds' bones and feathers, cord and hair which she found rattling on the church door was more unsettling. It took her several days to persuade John to tell her what it was. A 'witch's ladder' made to cause ill fortune, he finally confessed. Who was responsible?

## 20

Walking back to the Rectory late that afternoon as a full moon rose, she could just make out Hal the shepherd and his dog in the field rounding up the ewes; the bleats of the newborn lambs confirmed spring was coming. It was thrilling to think that tomorrow she would start the final panel. The panel would feature six stars cascading around a crowned Holy Lamb. She must get out in the field tomorrow, do some quick sketches of lambs so she could add some authentic details. It would be her best drawing yet.

Mildred's feet were solid with cold. Tonight she would warm them by the fire, have supper on a tray and wait for William to return. An added treat to find a letter from Elizabeth in the hall. Mildred settled down in the study to read.

*Dearest Mildred,*

*Mother's confusion is getting worse. She still thinks we live at the farm and wonders why Father has not left for work. The doctor says it is her age. We manage, give her buttons to sort into boxes and read to her. She is cheery enough. Thank goodness spring is on the way and we will be able to get out again.*

*I am so pleased that your work in the church is almost complete. As you know, I have been concerned about your safety working at that great height and in the cold of winter. I am less happy to hear, however, that you have not kept William informed about these silly signs that are left for you. They sound disturbing. Why have you not told him? If William finds out, he may be hurt that you have kept secrets from him.*

*However, I have never been able to persuade you of anything, my dear headstrong sister! So let me send love from us all and best wishes to William,*

*Elizabeth.*

Mildred rested her head back on a cushion. Why should she concern William with minor irritations over which he had no control? Having never had a husband, Elizabeth did not appreciate how much they needed to be managed. How tired she was tonight ...

What felt like minutes later, Mildred woke as the door was flung open. Rose looked distraught.

'Come, Ma'am, to the church, at once!'

Mildred heard shouting outside the window, perhaps Thomas's yelling, and then boots clattering across the yard.

'For goodness' sake. What's happening out there?' Mildred blearily reached for the boots which Rose held out, wincing as her chapped stiff fingers struggled with the buttons.

'Not sure, Ma'am, but Owen's run over to say we must come quick. Here's a shawl 'gainst the rain.'

Rose took a lamp and the women hurried towards the church. Mildred could see that one of the windows glowed blush-red.

PAMELA HOLMES

Her mind, still thick from sleep, was muddled. Why? Her sluggish legs refused to be chivvied and it felt like an age before they finally reached the church. There she saw the stableman Robert and Hal; they were grappling with a water butt, hauling it towards the church. What were they doing?

'Rose, we need help!' Both women joined in and, with two more sets of arms, the barrel was gradually manoeuvred into the church porch.

Hal pushed open the door. It was then she saw it. A fire around one of the scaffolding posts. Not a big one but everyone knew the greed of fire for life. Thomas and Owen Walton beat it with tools, their faces illuminated in the flames.

'We have the water!' Walton called, and now the barrel was on the firm surface of the church floor, it could be rolled more easily along on its metal edge.

Without speaking, Walton, Thomas, Rose, the stablemen, Hal and Mildred divided into two groups. Shoulder to shoulder in the heat, they formed a circle, scooping water from the barrel in one move, before tipping it into the flames in another. Like a country gig, their steps were quick; the briefest time in the face of the flame to empty the bucket or pot they held, then they swung away again for cooler air. The round began again with only the crackle of fire for music.

At first Owen had tried to restrain her but she shook him off. How strange it was to feel warm, she thought; she was usually freezing when in the church. She glanced quickly upwards. There were her angels. Peaceful golden faces gazed down, indifferent to the pandemonium below. Mildred dipped her flagon into the water. It was her turn again, and she stretched out to tip the water at the heart of the conflagration. Her hair sizzled and she stumbled. If Walton had not caught her belt from behind, she would have fallen.

One of the gardeners appeared pushing a wheelbarrow full

of soil. They stood aside to let him pass. Then, taking spades, he and Thomas began to scoop up the earth and to fling it over the flames. The damp soil fell in clumps like dead weights; thump, thump, mud and stones blanketed the fire. The other men joined in with their boots, stamping and stomping. The fire choked and sputtered, then died.

Everyone stood, shocked, in the now-dark church. An ember flared occasionally and was snuffed out with a boot. Already she could feel the chill on her damp neck as the cold crept back. All she longed to do now was to send the servants away, to be alone. She needed to sit and to weep and to consider the danger that had been averted. But responsibility must be answered.

Mildred said: 'How can I thank you all enough for what you have done?'

Her fellow firefighters looked relieved. 'You've saved our precious church, been brave and courageous. Is anyone injured?' And as she moved among them, checking for burns or scalds, she thanked each one again.

'Rose and Thomas, go back to the house,' she instructed. 'Fetch food and drink, will you? Cook will help. And the rest of you, please sit and rest.'

The men did as they were bid and sat against the wall in the dark or found places to perch. She knew it must feel strange for them to watch her moving while they waited, to see her lighting lamps and clearing a space for the food. Now the drama was over, they would perhaps prefer to leave for home too. But for her there was a simple comfort in the tasks of arrangement. Companionable to be with these generous people who had helped her, to know that together they had saved the church from burning. But she could not forget that there was someone in their midst, someone the men lived with or knew that had started the fire.

Crouching down, fearless now the fire posed no danger,

Mildred picked through the grimy mess of stones and soil and ash around the scaffolding. How had this fire started? She was relieved that they had protected the church but puzzled, too: who had done this?

'What has been going on?' William burst in the door, his face flushed. 'Who in God's name is responsible for this? Mildred, are you all right?'

Mildred touched his arm. 'I am fine. There was a fire, William, not a big one thankfully and we caught it before it threatened the church. So be patient, please; we will find out later how it started. The main thing is we are safe and the fire is out.' Rose arrived with a basket of food, Thomas with beer and Cook with more lamps.

'Thank you, set everything down over on that table.' Mildred turned to the men. 'Come and help yourselves. Owen, Thomas, Robert, the rest of you ...'

The strange evening continued; men eating and drinking in a place where some of them worshipped. She wondered what would be said in the village and what gossip and scandal Judy would start to spread.

William watched Mildred catering to his servants. Dressed in her extraordinary trousers, smuts streaked across her face, it was hard to contain his fury. If she had not set out on this ludicrous course of action to paint the ceiling, none of this would have happened. And tonight she had put her life at risk.

'Shall we inspect the damage?' he asked. He stiffened as she took his arm. He examined the scaffolding pole which had been in the flames. Its surface was scorched and blackened to shoulder height.

'It's almost burnt through at the base. It will have to be replaced,' he said bitterly. 'It will delay the work. How could this have happened, Mildred? And why in heaven's name did you risk your life to fight a fire? Why didn't you leave it for the men?'

'I can't answer these questions now.' He could hear her fighting the impulse to shout at him. 'I wonder that you ask me this, William, I do! For now, I am simply thankful that no one is hurt. Aren't you, William? And glad, very glad, that the church is not as damaged as I feared when I first saw the flames.'

William muddled the smouldering ashes with his shoe.

'Look at this! The remains of a box, and some rags, and sticks. It looks to me that it was started deliberately.' His voice was thick. 'We're going to find who did this – and mark my words, they will be punished!'

Pounding at the front door shocked them both awake. William's anger, not long abated, boiled up again, and his voice roared through the sleeping house as he thumped down the stairs to answer the door. Mildred peered out from between the bedroom curtains. Down below a group of men formed a circle around a struggling body. It must be a woman for she could see skirts blowing in the wind and hear a high-pitched mewling. Then Mary Fake's distraught face was caught in the light of William's lamp as he ran out of the house and Mildred knew at once that here was the person who hated her.

She remembered the last time she had seen Mary; at her daughter Martha's funeral. It was cruel that birds sang that day. Mary stood at side of the grave, her eyes fixed on the box that contained the once-fevered flesh of her little girl. As the coffin was lowered into the earth, she too slid to the soil, an unearthly gasp escaping her lips. Then Mary raised dead eyes to Mildred and shook her head in disbelief.

The memories made her shiver. Mildred dressed in her working clothes, aromatic with smoke, and limped as quickly as she could down the stairs. By the time she reached the front of the house, there was no sign anyone had been in the yard. But there were sounds from the stable block. She found two men standing outside one of the horse boxes; from inside it came the sound of raised voices and the snap of slapping and a woman's wail.

'Let me by,' Mildred pushed past the men. William and Harry Browne, the shopkeeper, were towering over Mary Fake. The woman cowered on the straw bedding, mud-streaked legs sticking out from her skirt, her feet bare and bleeding. Thomas, in the corner, looked terrified.

'I am asking you to answer my questions!' William sounded exasperated. 'I need to find out what happened. Speak up for yourself, can't you?'

'Get up, woman!' Browne angrily grabbed Mary's arm and yanked her upright, forcing her on to a stool. He held her with one hand and cuffed her across the head with the other. 'Speak to the Rector, answer his questions, you wretched thing! Was it you that started that fire?'

There was a whimper. Mary's face was smeared with tears and mucus. Her lip bled. Browne shook her hard. Her head flicked back and forth; there was an incoherent babble of words. 'You're a bad woman! You started the fire, didn't you? Admit it!?' And in disgust Browne flung her backwards. Mary slammed back on to the straw.

Mildred stepped forward. 'That's quite enough, Mr Browne,' she remonstrated. 'I am not sure this is helping. We must all remain calm.'

'I saw her tonight,' the man spluttered. 'I was out snaring rabbits with some others. We wondered what a woman was doing out after dark. Snared her instead, easy as anything. Found matches in her pocket.' Mildred could smell alcohol on his breath. 'The publican told us about that fire and we knew it was her what did it. Fetched her up to the Rector straightaway.'

'Thank you for that, Mr Browne, we are most grateful for your help. Now, please leave us.' Mildred placed herself between the man and Mary.

'And will you call for the magistrate? This woman must be tried!' Browne pointed an accusing finger.

'We will consider it, of course. Now thank you all for your help. Please leave.'

None of the men moved. Mildred insisted: 'Must I say it again? Good night. Call by the Fakes' cottage, if you would be so kind. Check that Seth, Mary's husband or a neighbour is there with the children. Mr Browne – Mrs Browne will want you back home. I am sure she will be worried.'

The men filed out. Mildred gestured to Thomas.

'Ask Rose to bring warm water and some rags. A shot of brandy and some blankets.' The boy raced out, seemingly grateful to escape.

'But if she is the culprit, we need to ...' said William.

'This is not the way to find out. Frighten the woman half to death? Let her calm down first. Imagine being captured by *that* group of men.'

Mildred knelt down by the woman who was moaning, and in a low dispassionate voice said: 'Mary, you are safe now. Rose will tend to your wounds presently. You will spend the night here. We will wait nearby until Rose comes.'

Mildred instructed the two men to stand outside the stall to guard Mary, then she and William went along the stable block to find somewhere private. Horses shifted in their stables, their breath scenting the air. They went into the tack room with its soothing smell of soaped leather. William sat on a chair and she leaned back against him with a sigh.

'What a terrible night.' William rubbed his eyes. 'Shall I send for the constable now? I rather doubt he will be sober at this time if he's still awake, but one can always hope.'

'I think we should wait 'til morning, don't you? He can inform the magistrate and we can consider what to do. But are we going to press a case? For what reason? It may end up in the assizes court.'

'The church could have burnt down. It came close to a disaster,' William retorted.

'It was only a small fire in the end, William. I know we were lucky that the whole place didn't catch, you're right. But do we *know* it's Mary? Browne is convinced she started it but ...'

'Seems very much like he's right. Matches in her pocket, found out after dark. Why wasn't she at home with her children? It doesn't look good.'

'Did you see her lip, William? It was cut and bleeding. If one of those men has taken it on himself to ...'

'Perhaps she fell when she was running?'

'Perhaps she did. But if I find out that one of them has raised his hand to her, he will not go unpunished either.' Mildred's annoyance was swamped by a yawn. 'Let's wait for morning then. My darling, we really should get to bed. Rose will attend Mary and they'll be safe in the stable guarded by the men.'

# 21

C haotic dreams disturbed her sleep. Her angels were flushed and feverish, beseeching her for help. But she could not reach them and could only watch as their golden wings smouldered and dripped and then they floated away. Mildred woke, shivering and anxious. Images from the previous night's drama blotted out any sense of proportion. She felt terrified again; how near it had come to her losing everything, how hard she had struggled to create her angels.

Needing comfort, she reached for William's hands, settled them on her breasts and arched back against his body. She wrapped her feet around his knees, woke him with her insistent pressing and weaving against his body. Sleepily his hands moved down to her hips and now he was awake to her. The familiar pressure of his loins against her rump as he took his slow pleasure brought her ease. Then she twisted around to tuck her head under his chin and fell soundly back to sleep.

'Mr Holland and I will see your sister this morning,' Mildred said coldly when Rose brought breakfast in the next morning. 'Before we call for the constable, we will talk to her. Did you dress her wounds? Has Mary had any sleep at all, do you know?'

'I cleaned her cuts up last night, and the bruises, then I give her some soup. The guards said she was crying most of the night.'

From her puffy eyes, it was obvious Rose had been crying, too. 'Before you go, Mrs Holland, could I have a word, please?'

'What is it, Rose?'

'Thank you, Ma'am. It's about Mary.' Rose closed the door. 'I was with her last night, washed her an' that, calmed her down a bit. She talked. It were hard to make sense of everything what she said, but she confessed it. It were her what did it ... started the fire an' all.'

Rose dropped to her knees. Her face was distraught; Mildred could smell the girl's acrid breath. 'Be merciful to her, Ma'am. She's not been right since Martha died. She's wrong, I know, but she thinks you could've saved the girl. I tell her you done your best, that the fever was too strong. But she broods, Mrs Holland, she broods.'

'Why are you telling me this, Rose? I did my best to save Martha. There was nothing I could do.'

'And the baby, it keeps her up all the time and she's so tired, she don't think straight.'

'That's no excuse to take revenge and start a fire in the church, Rose! Surely you can see that? If she's admitted it, she must take responsibility for what she has done.'

Rose howled, pressed herself to Mildred's skirt. 'But Ma'am, if you call the constable, she'll be taken away, prison, maybe worse. Her children, Ma'am, what will they do if she's not there to look after them?'

Mildred gulped. She pushed Rose away.

'How dare you speak to me of this? Is losing a child an excuse for doing wrong? Perhaps she should have thought of this before causing this trouble. Get up at once! Return to your duties!'

Rose fled the room. Mildred was stunned. This was intolerable. That a servant should make representations to her in the face of her sister's blatant guilt. She wanted to smash something. Unable to contain her agitation, she fled for the church.

It was quiet in there, smoke-scented. Apart from one burnt scaffolding pole, there was no evidence there had been a fire. Order had been restored. Things were as they had been when she had finished painting yesterday. She looked up. Above the scaffolding, she could see the ceiling and her angels painted on it. They were serene, looked down with equanimity; unperturbed by the drama of the night before. Mildred began to cry; first tears of anger but soon they became tears of relief.

With that came a resolution, a clarity that had eluded her during the night. When the natural order is violated and a child dies, it is confirmation that there is no order in the world. Fairness cannot be assumed or expected. What logic then to punish wrongdoing? Did the one inevitably follow the other? She said a prayer and walked slowly back to the Rectory.

William was in the parlour. Mildred took his hand.

'My dear, Rose spoke to me this morning. She says that Mary has confessed to starting the fire. Rose says her sister has never recovered from Martha's death and in some way blames me for it. Of course that's nonsense, I know, but Mary's been low and unhappy, Rose says, since her last baby's birth. Her husband Seth is rarely around, only long enough to impregnate her, so she's desperate and gets little help from him. William, I have considered this carefully. I have prayed to God and I want you to listen. I am not willing to take this episode any further. I am not going to expose this woman to the force of the law. What Mary needs is a doctor, not incarceration.'

'What?' William exploded. 'You're suggesting we don't seek retribution, not punish her?'

'She's punished enough already. The woman is half mad with grief. She blames me for Martha's death. We both know about that – the desire to apportion blame. What would we gain from taking her to the law? The church has survived. No one was hurt.'

'You might have been injured, Millie, your life was in danger!'

'It benefits no one if Mary is punished. But it harms her children for certain. We must be merciful, William.'

William shook his head. She went on: 'We can't consider spoiling everything we've done in the parish and in the church, by taking out an action against Mary Fake. It's not what we want, William. We want to bring harmony to Huntingfield, not division. Let's agree we will *help* Mary, not harm her. And carry on with what we've set out to do.'

The chancel ceiling is complete. Where once plain wooden rafters arched above the heads of earthbound mortals, now painted golden-crowned angels cover an azure star-filled sky. Decorated borders of pattern and colour make the eyes dance and the spirits soar. A sense of glory and glamour dominates. In a week's time, the first service in St Mary's for six months will take place.

Although Mildred is dressed for work, she does not take the familiar path across the churchyard past the slumping headstones and into the church. The sun, warm today for the first time this year, shines across the brown fields tempting the sleeping plants to trust that spring has come. She stands at her bedroom window, straining to hear the first sounds of a cart coming up the lane. For today Mr Spall of Norwich is expected. It is an extraordinary sight. Up the long Rectory drive from the lane are two carts of carved wooden angels. Vast wingspans make methodical arrangement of the figures impossible. One angel sprawls in an ungainly pose over another which lies submerged beneath the wings of a third. The beatific expressions of the passengers remain unsullied. None register the indignity of their position. The team of horses strains to pull its heavy angelic load.

Mildred hurries out and clucks like an anxious hen as each statue is lifted down to earth. She has work to do for each angel must be decorated. They are spread across the lawn in a heavenly group. Glue is smoothed over the grained surface of each angel's body. With deliberate care, books of gold leaf are lifted from the heavy leather pouches in which they have travelled from London. These glittering pages reveal no stories but magic dances on their mirrored surfaces. A gentle breeze could tear the shiny sheets from uncertain fingers, so fine and thinly beaten are they. Only the heat from Mildred's hand makes the gold leaf rise like a magic carpet from the books of gold. A sheet is then coaxed flat to lie on the sticky surface of carved wing, curl of hair or crenulation of crown. With smoothing and stroking, it is persuaded to settle and bind. With brush and cloth, Mildred then burnishes each sheet until it shimmers. Like an alchemist, she transforms wood into gold.

Now her angels are ready. The winches are securely in position. Mildred bids each darling figure farewell as it flies upward like a golden bird to find its home at the end of a roof beam; from where it will sit serene, to survey all who worship below.

## 22

Most of the village were in the wood that morning, dressed in their Sunday best. In brown, grey and black they merged into the background; it was as though the trees were moving. The subdued crowd pressed forward, fixed on its destination. Little conversation, just the odd murmur or acknowledgement of an acquaintance; the swish of a sappy twig or the rustle of a dry leaf as it was brushed by leg or skirt; the whispers of children. Even the birds were quiet.

William stood at the open church door, smiling as his parishioners streamed in at the gate, nodding at those he knew well and those he barely recognised. All were coming to the church, the first service to be held in over six months, intrigued to see what rumours suggested the mistress of the Rectory had done to their church and its ceiling.

People entered the building and immediately looked up. Most gasped when they saw for the first time the kaleidoscope of colour that now spread across the ceiling. They hurried down to the chancel steps, faces uplifted, not daring to go any further; this was where the wealthy families sat and from where the Rector would later address them. The aisle quickly bottled up as more people arrived, piling and stumbling into those who had stopped midway to gaze up at the frescos. Angels holding emblems of the Passion of Christ – the cross, the crown of thorns, the hammer and the nails. Two pelicans pecking at their white breasts, feeding their young on the blood that trickled out. Gothic lettering on scrolls of religious verses, shields and banners. And smiling down from the rafters, golden-crowned angels.

The entrance became jammed. People pressed in at the door, craning their necks over a neighbour's shoulder to see what was causing the bottleneck. A murmur rumbled to disquiet and when someone called out 'Let us in!' there was a surge. People gushed through the door; an old man tripped and fell over. He remained on his knees, staring open-mouthed at the scene above him.

'Take care, be calm!' called William.

Now people clambered on to pews or lifted children so they could see over the head of a neighbour. Whispering to each other, pointing and gesturing, the few who could read did so for those who were unable to decipher the holy script.

No one noticed Mildred at the back of the church. In the gloom under the west window she paced, one glove off, biting at her nail, watchful, trying to judge the verdict of the crowd. What were the village folk thinking? What were they saying? She felt ludicrous with uncertainty. Would they be angry with what she had done to their little church?

Then out of the melee appeared Ann, walking towards her with arms outstretched in welcome as if the two had met only last week. In a pink-striped coat and ribboned bonnet, Ann grinned. Not a shadow of their quarrel tainted her face. 'Mildred, my dear, it looks beautiful, the church is quite stunning. You have amazed me. I've brought you these. Look at what you've done!'

'Ann? It's so good to see you here. I wasn't expecting ... Thank you, yes, for coming. The violets are for me? Oh thank you. How are the children, and Richard?'

A warm embrace can melt the stiffest posture. 'Mildred, we're all here, the whole family. We couldn't miss the opening of the church. It's been how long? Ages, almost a year and ...'

Edward loomed out of the shadow and stepped between them. 'You must sit, Mildred. Here, come.' And taking her elbow, he guided her over to a chair set at the back of the church. He pulled out a handkerchief and with what Mildred thought an overly-dramatic flick of the wrist, polished the seat where she would sit.

She sniffed the posy of tiny purple flowers. 'Join me, will you Ann? It is good to see you here. You're looking well.' As for herself, Mildred was taut with trepidation.

'Thank you, my dear, we are all content. It's marvellous, Mildred, truly stunning!' Ann whispered.

Gradually people found places to sit or they squeezed into a space around the edge of the church. William waited on the chancel steps for people to settle. Then his sonorous voice boomed out and the service started. The rituals of prayer, the reading and sermon were soothing and Mildred's breathing gradually steadied. A wave of exhaustion washed through her; she felt sleepy, her limbs heavy, she stifled a yawn. Grateful for a rousing hymn, she stole a sideways glance at Ann. The woman sang with gusto, her head thrust back, her mouth open wide. Why had she come? What about their quarrel? Just in front of them sat Edward. He followed the service sheet, his lips barely moving. He seemed to sense her eyes and turned around; the corners of his mouth twitched. She looked away. Not until the congregation began the final hymn did she dare to lift her eyes up again. Up to the ceiling, the high place where she had stood for so many dark and cold months.

'Tell me again what it looks like,' said Judy bossily. 'Prop up my pillows, will you, and tell me again.'

It was the third time Rose had described the church renovations. She had done her best to give an account of what had been done but it was not enough for Judy, as though Judy could not accept that so much had happened over which she'd had no influence.

'New seats, you say? What are they made of? What's on the ceiling?'

'Pictures of angels. John explained it to me, what it all means,' said Rose. 'There's a cross and the hammer and nails and the angels from the story of the crucifixion. And a bird, a big white bird what's feeding her young with blood, ugh. Words on scrolls too but I can't remember what they say, sayings from the Bible, I think. And colour, bright colour everywhere, all beautiful, and borders around the top of the wall, all decorated. And in some parts, real gold. I were shocked at first. It looks so different an' not what we're used to at all.'

Judy said: 'How could she do it? How did she *know* how to paint like that? It's a tall building, dangerous, for that one weak woman.'

'And statues, too, hanging off the beams, angels lookin' down with their big wings like they'll fly away. John says they may have been angels there in the church in times past.'

A sense of power, knowing about things that Judy did not, was delicious. It made Rose almost boastful.

'There, I've told you what I've seen, Judy, and I've done me best and it's no good asking me again for I'll only tell you the same.'

Rose retreated to the window, half turned away. Both women were silent.

Then Judy whined: 'Well I think it's terrible, changing our church like that. Who gave her the right to do it, I'd like to know? It was better when it was plain and simple.'

'You've not seen it, Judy. If you'd like to come and see it for yourself, I'll push you there, in one of John's chairs with wheels. I'm sure I could manage it. You might like it.'

'I very much doubt that!' Judy spat back. 'There's no way that I am leaving this bed to see anything that woman has done to ruin our church!'

Sounds of voices and laughter spilled out from a passing carriage as it rattled past the Scotts' cottage. 'Visitors for the church, I'd say,' Judy threw herself back against the pillow. 'It's causing a terrible racket, all those carriages rolling through the village, people coming here, disturbing the peace.'

'Well, it's bringing money into the village,' Rose said flatly. 'At the shop, the post office, even the tailor says he's had more trade. People want tea and refreshments, gifts, trinkets. They're going to do tea at the tavern and Mrs Lambert is going to start to offer bed and board, so if people want to stay ...'

'Stay? In her house? I've never heard anything so ridiculous. Laundry Cottage?' Judy straightened the bed cover, almost shouting. 'What has that Holland woman done to our village?'

Ned hurried into the bedroom, his white hair bouncing as he hobbled over to his wife's bedside. 'Calm yourself, my love. It's not good for you to get upset now.' He straightened her coverlet and started to plump her pillows.

'I'm perfectly fine, leave me be, Ned!' she hissed, pushing him away angrily. 'Have you heard this ridiculous news? People might be staying at the Lamberts' so they can see the church, painted up like a fairground!'

'People are saying it's good for the village,' added Rose firmly. 'People are talking a lot of nonsense,' retorted Judy.

## 23

1860 THREE DAYS LATER

A note was brought to the Rectory. Mildred recognised Ann's handwriting immediately. But the envelope lay on the hall table for several hours before Mildred picked it up. Something held her back, pride perhaps, a sense that opening it was an admission that she had agreed to be friends again. Part of her was eager to read it but there was another part of her that remained aggrieved; wounded that Ann had abandoned her apparently so carelessly.

Despite this equivocation, two days later she drove herself to the Owens' house. Passing through the village, she noticed several traps outside the tavern and a group of well-dressed people milling about the older Lambert boy. Thomas had told her that villagers were already offering tours of the church.

A gibbering bird flew out of the hedge, startling Mildred and her horse. Did he feel nervy too? She ran her hand down the cloth of a new jacket and tucked a lace scarf in round her collar. She must look her best for this visit.

Ann greeted her at the door. It was oddly familiar; the kiss on the cheek, the walk past the nursery, a wave to the older girls who broke off from their lessons to give her a hug. Ann waited patiently as Mildred kissed Helen and handed the chubby two-year-old back to the nursemaid. Neither women spoke as they crossed the lawn and went into the garden house. Ann shut the door and gestured Mildred should sit.

'I owe you an explanation, and I hope you can find it in yourself to forgive me.' Ann's manner was collected but the high colour of usually-pale cheeks suggested she was agitated. 'I heard about the fire,' she went on. 'William told Richard about it after the service on Sunday. Terrifying. After that, I knew I couldn't keep my secret any longer.'

Mildred wiped her forehead. Her jacket was too heavy for this warm weather. She pulled off her scarf and gloves.

'I had to tell you what I'd done. I hope you can forgive me,' Ann was restless. She paced over to the window. Beyond her, Mildred could see flashes of yellow; the canaries were flying about their cage.

Ann said solemnly: 'It was me that left those silly signs at the church.'

Mildred stared at her in disbelief. Ann went on: 'I was trying to warn you off painting the ceiling. I know it was wrong of me but I was angry ...'

'It was *you*?' Mildred shook her head. 'You who left that vile bottle of nails, that odd tangle of feathers and bones?'

'Yes,' Ann nodded solemnly. 'To warn you.'

'To warn me ... of what? What were you trying to stop me doing?'

'I didn't start the fire, though. That was someone else. I would never have done that! Risk destroying things, oh no, I only wanted to frighten you. You see, I thought what you were doing was too dangerous.'

'Dangerous. What do you mean? That I might fall?' Mildred flushed with anger.

'Not that kind of danger.'

'You're not making sense, Ann. What do you mean?'

Ann sat down; she looked wretched. 'There's something I've never told you. About my past.' Ann's voice was almost inaudible. Mildred leant forward to catch her words. 'Because I'm ashamed about it. I'd much rather you didn't know. But I must tell you, and I pray you will understand why I did what I did.'

A bead of sweat rolled down Mildred's temple.

Ann said: 'When I was younger, I had a son. I wasn't married to Richard at that time. I ... I wasn't married to anyone. It was in Sussex. I was living in Sussex with a painter ... as his mistress.' She glimpsed up at Mildred. 'I lived there, did my work, my stained glass. I got several commissions, some good ones. I loved being where I was and I was happy. My family didn't know the situation, of course; they thought I lodged with a respectable family. But I became pregnant and my lover and ... he didn't want ... he abandoned me.'

Ann hung her head.

'My family threatened to disown me when I told them. They couldn't accept what had happened – they were going to cut me off! I had already met Richard through another family in the village where I lived with my ... painter. Richard was their son. He'd come back to start a local law practice. His parents didn't approve but Richard was in love with me, had been for some time. He knew my situation. He spoke to my family and offered to marry me, as long as I gave the child away. My parents were so grateful, relieved, that the scandal could be kept secret. They paid for me to go to a convent where I could finish pregnancy, have my baby. I gave birth there, to a beautiful angelic boy. A few days after his birth, it was arranged for him to be taken away ...' Tears filled Ann's eyes.

Mildred felt nauseous; from heat or shock, she didn't know which. She put out her hand towards her friend. 'Oh Ann, I'm so sorry. This is tragic. To lose a baby. You poor dear woman. There must have been unbearable pressure on you, an unmarried mother.' She wiped her upper lip and asked gently, 'Do you know where your son is now?'

'I don't know where he is or even if he's still alive. I called him Remi. He'd be a young man by now, almost sixteen. How I would love to see him!'

Neither woman spoke for some minutes. Then Mildred asked: 'Why couldn't you take the commission for the St Mary's window. I still don't understand that.'

'Yes, there's more,' Ann voice was deadpan. 'The other stipulation Richard made was that I should give up my life as an artist. He thinks that kind of life can corrupt those who are not morally strong – women like me, vulnerable women. That's why I could not take on the commission you offered. I agreed with him that I would never work like that again. Do you see? Of course I wanted to do it – but I gave him my word.'

Mildred was appalled. Did Richard suspect she, Mildred, had a poor moral character because she had painted a church ceiling? 'I find that extraordinarily difficult to understand,' she said as diplomatically as she could. Did he think that art corrupted women or vice versa?

'It was part of his bargain,' Ann went on. 'I had no choice but to accept it. But Richard has watched William deal with your wishes, he's seen how your husband feels about your work and what you've achieved. He knows that William is proud of you and supports you. I think Richard's starting to see things differently now, at least where other women are concerned. But I knew he wouldn't be happy about *me* accepting the work. I know my husband.'

'But why those silly signs?' Mildred was still irritated with Ann and flummoxed by what she had admitted to doing.

'It was stupid of me, I know, Mildred. But I was jealous. Why should you be able to work if I could not? It didn't seem fair.'

Ann pushed open the garden room door with her shoe; a little breeze drifted in, and the birdsong of the canaries. How paradoxical, Mildred thought. Ann couldn't work because she had had a baby, while Mildred knew that if she had become pregnant, her passion to paint might never have become the obsession that it had.

'I feared for you, too.' Ann lowered her voice to a whisper. 'When I saw Edward Blackburne and the way he felt about you, I wanted to stop it. I didn't trust him. I was worried that he might lead you astray ... as I had been.'

Mildred laughed ruefully. 'So you left those objects thinking they would scare me? Did you honestly think I would be susceptible to some half-baked witchcraft?'

'You've too much sense for that, I know,' Ann replied unhappily. She continued to speak as she moved around the garden room, picked up a shawl that had been discarded on a chair. 'I suppose I got carried away, festering here on my own. I just wanted to stop you, Mildred. I remembered you'd said some of the villagers thought you were a witch. Leaving amulets around the place seemed the sort of thing they might do. And you'd never have suspected me.'

Ann went outside and draped the shawl over the canaries' cage. Their singing stopped almost immediately. Standing in the doorway, she continued: 'I'm sorry, Mildred. I feel I have betrayed you. Can you forgive me? It was right for you to paint the ceiling. Seeing it on Sunday proved it. The church is beautiful. What can I say? I was overwhelmed and so was Richard. I'm just so glad that I didn't stop you!'

## 24

1860 LATER THAT DAY

'She's a complex creature. When I first met Ann, she seemed delightfully straightforward. More interesting than the other women in the area, yes, but I'd no idea she would have such a sad troubled tale. As for her risqué past, well that was a complete shock!'

William peered quizzically over his glass at his wife. They were having dinner, had just finished the soup and were eating the chicken fricassee that Rose had served.

'Vegetables, Millie? I see that you are more than a little fascinated by her revelations. I may scold my wife for being curious.' He poured her another glass of wine. 'But instead I commend her for being a good friend. Ann's taken you into her confidence. It must be a great relief to her that someone else knows her past. It's a very sad tale. As we only too well know, the Lord tests us in many ways. We must just be grateful that Ann was rescued by Richard from her difficult situation and is now living a modest and regular Christian life.'

William's reaction did not surprise Mildred. He always forgave people and rarely judged them. He left *that* for God, he told her. It was the same with Mary Fake. He'd agreed that they would not seek retribution or punish the woman. She supposed that was what made him a good parish priest.

'And Ann does not know whether or not her child is alive or dead. That must be very hard,' she added.

'We will pray for Ann and for all her children. And petition that we and those we love are not tempted to stray from the right path.' William patted his mouth with a napkin. 'We must congratulate Cook on that dish. Perhaps it's something to serve for lunch on Sunday? It's very good news that you and Ann are friends again. I'm so pleased.'

'As am I, William. I missed her very much,' Mildred knew how much she meant this. 'It's been a strange and painful process getting to know Ann, but I think I'll understand her better now.'

'Will the Owens be coming to the service?' William asked.

The Bishop had agreed to preside over the Sunday service at St Mary's and to lead special prayers of thanks for the newly-opened church. Local dignitaries and clergy from the diocese had been invited to lunch at the Rectory. William hoped Mildred would enjoy the accolades that were bound to be expressed by everyone who came. But he knew she was not in a steady state of mind. The energy and passion which had inured her to the cold hours of painting had dissipated like mist now the work was complete, leaving her deflated and exhausted. He saw her doubt every compliment, watched her listening to what people said, hearing criticisms where none were intended. Thank goodness the Bishop was supportive. His prayers would certainly help. She needed a rest; he must take her away on a holiday.

～

Anxiety woke William early next morning. He sensed immediately his wife was not beside him in the bed. With an apology to God for missing prayers, he dressed quickly. It was too early even for the servants to be awake. Reckoning she might have gone to the church, William hurried across the soggy graveyard. Clouds sagged. The lamp glowed under his umbrella. As soon as the door opened, he knew the church was empty, empty at least of living souls, even if it was alive with coloured images and golden angels which he could just make out above him. He had not been alone in the church since Mildred had finished her work. Shaking off the worst of the rain, he walked up to the chancel and knelt down.

William always thought best on his knees. He remembered the doubts he had harboured as he watched her dress each day in her trousers and queer hat. He had dealt with these qualms in the same way in which he managed his battles with all spiritual doubt. Long ago he had accepted that for him, victorious Christian life was not having his questions answered but learning to live with them. He abandoned the view that evidence constituted the essential foundation for faith; he placed his trust in prayer and parish work to prevent dilemmas becoming destructive doubts. It had not been easy, however, to deal with the scepticism of some such as Sydney Pegler.

'A madcap scheme, Mildred painting the church, don't you think William?' Sydney said one night at dinner in Darsham. 'Let's be honest, William, it's not a job for a woman, is it? You've married a plucky one and I can see she is determined. But do we really think she can manage it?'

William had loyally defended his wife while secretly wondering if Sydney wasn't right. Others had spoken to him more forcefully about their concerns and he had needed a certain amount of bravado to deal with their hostility. Deep down, William questioned whether Mildred would be able manage it. How wrong they had all been. Above him was the evidence of her triumph. There was more than a twinge of guilt mixed with his pride as he climbed back to his feet.

Dawn light slipped in at the east window. William left the church. The wind whipped the last of the blossom from the trees; they scattered like snowflakes. It reminded him of a wonderful walk with Mildred in the snow in Berne; the delicious chocolate they drank in a tiny café afterwards, her face flushed with happiness and warmth. He hurried over to the stables. As he expected she was in the studio curled up in a blanket on a sofa. Her face was hidden in dishevelled hair. The stove was unlit. Gusts of rain rattled the windows like chattering teeth.

'Millie, what are you doing here?' He knelt down, pushed the hair from her eyes and stroked her cheek.

She looked up wearily. 'I couldn't sleep, William. I woke early and didn't want to disturb you and ... I've been thinking.' He saw an expression he had learnt to distrust; one he recognised from the day she wanted to climb to see the angels in that Southwold church. Her eyes a little too shiny, her breathing uneven, shallow.

'We need to do more, William. We need to complete the decoration so the whole church is painted. Have you seen this?' She rallied herself to sit up. 'It's the new William Morris Company catalogue. There are some glorious designs. Look at that! It would suit a carpet in the ...' She flicked rapidly through the pages.

'But we have done what we planned to do, Millie, and it looks stunning!'

'We cannot leave it as it is. It's incomplete.'

'What do you mean incomplete? What else needs to be done?'

'The nave. I need to complete the whole ceiling, not half of it. It doesn't look right, only one part being painted.'

She was agitated. He had seen this before. He shook his head. 'But it would take you ages, who knows, even years!'

'I know, I know, but I feel … I feel I must do it. I've come up with some ideas.'

She sprang up as though now brimming with energy. She gathered scrolls of papers covered with drawings and sketches and spread them out triumphantly on the floor. 'Come and see, my darling, here. For the nave ceiling, I've worked up these designs. What do you think?'

Her eyes were on his face, restless, searching, looking at him but not connecting somehow. She was elsewhere, in her imagination, envisaging herself back on the scaffolding, he suspected. Mildred tugged at his sleeve.

'Don't you see, William? I'll be better prepared this time, and everyone will like it.' She was whispering, talking more to herself than to him. 'John will be quicker and I know how to apply the paint. I'll work in short intensive bursts so it's not so tiring and then they will see …'

She turned to study her sketches again, began to scrabble through them. He felt furious. He wanted to grab her shoulders and shake her! She would make herself ill if she took on painting the whole ceiling. It wouldn't be possible to hold a service there for years – where would the villagers worship? She had done a marvellous job, of that there was no doubt but enough was enough!

Around the room lay the scattered evidence of her preparation. Papers, scrolls, swatches, brushes, books, pens, paints, drawings, pins, hammers; paraphernalia she was rifling through in excitement. He perched on a stool, dejected. She was so stubborn. He knew in his heart that when she wanted something enough, she would, eventually, persuade him to agree. He knew she would get her way. The infuriating thing was she knew it too.

'Can't we just carry on as we are for the time being, Mildred? My dear, the Bishop will be down at breakfast shortly. You know he is giving the service today. Let's get back to the house and attend to our guest, to our responsibilities!'

At this remark, she froze. 'Responsibility? To whom? You question that! Do I not have responsibility to myself, also, husband? The paint. I miss it, William, I miss it. The smell, the look, the smooth, shiny touch of it. It is part of me, it is on me, it is *in* me. Haven't you realised that yet?'

## 25

'You must persuade him.' Edward spoke with such conviction she felt pinned against the sofa. He stood against the fire, his black form outlined in a glow of red. He's blocking out my light and the heat, she thought.

'You have done a wonderful job. But the work is not finished. You know that.' He fixed her with his eyes. 'You are a remarkable woman and a committed artist.'

'I'm an amateur painter,' she retorted.

'But a good one, Mildred! You must persuade William to pay for the final stage. You can't leave it undone ... half-finished. It doesn't do you credit.'

'It's not about me.'

'People are travelling from all over the country to see your work. I've seen it, written about in journals – people talk about what we've done in London!'

'I have discussed it with William.'

He seemed to slide imperceptibly closer without moving his feet. 'And I will be here to assist you as before.' She could feel his body heat; his voice was thick. 'I will be here, advising you, helping you. Persuade him you need the money and then we ... you can get on with this important work.'

He hovered over her, dominated her, his glittering eyes peering out from under dark eyebrows. She became mesmerised by his lips, slipping over his teeth as he talked. His hand moved out towards her. She felt his finger and thumb circle her wrist and the slow pull as he lowered her hand away from her mouth. 'The Huntingfield Paintress ...'

Suddenly, she snapped. Standing up quickly, almost pushing into him, she drew herself up straight. 'That's enough, Edward,' she hissed. 'Press me no more. I will talk to William and we, *we* will decide together if and when we go on with the work!'

She swerved roughly past him and moved towards the side table. Now free of him, she felt cold and fierce. 'Thank you for all that you've done for us. We are most grateful. But we do not need your services any longer!'

She rang the bell hard. 'It is a shame you cannot stay for tea, Edward. But William will understand that you must be on your way. Ah, Rose. Will you bring in the tea? But none for Mr Blackburne. He has decided he must leave immediately. Get his coat and hat, will you?'

Later that day, a labourer told his wife – who told Judy – that Mildred's trap was seen racing along the lane in the direction of the sea. Several hours passed before the trap returned, the horse was white with sweat. Something had unsettled the vicar's wife but none of Judy's spies could confirm the cause.

Mildred was incandescent with rage. How dare Edward suggest she must 'persuade' William to fund her work, as though he was a pawn in a vainglorious scheme which indulged her vanity? His remark about the church 'being talked about in London' made her furious. Did he think she had stood on those cold, hard boards to be admired? His remarks sullied her creation.

Now she had escaped Edward. Once he had had some influence with her, it was true, but no longer. He was not entirely to blame; she had needed him and used him. He had released something in her, an untrammelled rush of will. But now she would do it on her own. For she had persuaded William that she would finish painting the rest of St Mary's church ceiling.

Three men from the village, sailors in the merchant navy on leave from their ships docked at Ipswich, developed the symptoms of that most feared disease – cholera. Vomiting, sickness, stomach cramps and violent, fishy-smelling diarrhoea, these symptoms caused terror. News quickly spread around the area – cholera in Huntingfield – and people from outlying cottages and farms stopped coming to the village; even the doctor refused to visit for what could he do? The village was quiet with quarantine.

As soon as Mildred heard the news, she took food and supplies to the men's families.

'It gave me a chance to see what is going on in those households,' she told William later that day. 'It was appalling. The women use the same bucket to dispose of the soiled linen as they carry drinking water in for the family. No one washes after they've touched the sick man. They simply have no idea about infection. Cholera is going to spread!'

Mildred and William believed in the views of Dr John Snow. He had made a study of a Soho water pump and collected details of infection among those drinking water from it. His proposal that faeces-contaminated water caused the disease was gradually gaining acceptance, and his evidence, published in one of the scientific journals they read, was convincing enough to persuade one local council to disable the well pump by removing its handle.

'The villagers still believe it's caused by "bad air" or miasma. It's what they've always thought,' replied William resignedly. 'And it's not going to be easy to persuade them otherwise. Especially when the local doctor agrees.'

'We have to do something, William, the disease could devastate the village. We have to teach them about boiling water, hand washing, to discard soiled clothes ... But how can we make them listen?'

William shook his head. 'You know what they'll say. It's just a new-fangled theory from London. They're suspicious of things they don't understand.'

'I tried talking to some other women living nearby. Knocked on their doors, but there was the usual mistrust. They were willing enough to take the food I offered but when I tried to talk about clean water, soap, vinegar and so on, they simply shut the door on me. Some were polite, others less so. It's maddening.' She turned to her husband. 'There's only one person who can help – Judy Scott. I'm going to have to ask for the support of that ... that horrible woman.'

William smiled. 'Surely my brave wife is not afraid of a white-haired bed-bound old lady?'

~

Judy was sitting up in bed, her white collar neatly tied, sheets pulled tight, looking fresh. Her expression soured as Ned ushered Mildred into the bedroom.

'Good day, Mrs Holland,' she said with pursed lips. She gestured that Mildred should sit in the chair at the bedside.

'Thank you. Good morning to you. I trust you are well?'

'I struggle on,' Judy replied.

'The Rector sends his regards. Let me get to the point, Judy. As you are aware, there is cholera in three village families, and we must all do everything possible to prevent it spreading. I need your help, your support in order to save Huntingfield.'

Imperceptibly, Judy sat up a little straighter. 'Pray explain.'

'I've brought you this article written by a Dr Snow from London. He has a theory about the spread of cholera; that it happens through tainted, dirty water. Our local doctor may not agree, I know that. But in Snow's opinion, and a local council has taken action in the light of his work, further infections can be prevented if some simple rules about cleanliness are strictly followed. I *must* convince the village women to take these measures. If you, with your influence, would back me up, we could save the village.'

Judy looked momentarily placated, then suspicious as Mildred held out a sheet of paper.

'May I leave this with you?' Judy accepted it gingerly.

Mildred could see the woman was torn between wishing to disrupt anything in which Mildred was involved and the respect that was being shown to her intelligence and influence.

'It's come to my notice that you've been visiting the sick families,' Judy said coolly. 'I agree to read the article and then I'll decide.'

Mildred nodded her thanks and was making to leave when Judy said: 'I understand the church ceiling is splendid, Mrs Holland, and that it is well regarded by many visitors. Of course, I have not seen it myself. But if what others say is true, I must congratulate you on your work.'

Mildred was flabbergasted. She turned around. Was this a new side of Judy; had she decided to be friendly?

'Thank you,' Mildred said warmly. 'Perhaps one day we'll

find a way to take you to the church so you can see for yourself.' There was a pause. In Judy's pink and white, almost wrinkleless face, sat two hard eyes. 'But I hear that it's only partly done,' she said, 'painted where the Huntingfield family have their seat ... the pew, I think they call it? The part where the *fine* families sit, not the common people. Is that so, Mrs Holland? Yet I understand from the Scriptures, what I read if I'm not mistaken, is that God loves us all equally. So why has the ceiling not been done for the likes of us?'

The word went out through the village that Mrs Holland's advice should be followed. Over the next days, as Mildred visited the houses of the sick men as well as other Huntingfield dwellings, she found her instructions were grudgingly accepted. The women took her instructions about boiling water for drinking and washing. They accepted the clean rags and the soap she gave them, scrubbed out their buckets and bowls. Strange how contented Mildred felt as she walked through the deserted village or rode on horseback to one of the outlying cottages. Like an evangelist, she carried her message of cleanliness. It was not the same happiness she felt when she looked at the church ceiling and saw her angels. Not the joy she felt when in her studio and a new design emerged magically from the tip of her pen. But a contentment nevertheless; a feeling of competence that she could be of use to these frightened ill-informed people.

The three sailors died from cholera. The stillness which had lain like a thick blanket over the fields of Huntingfield was broken by the banging of nail into wood as coffins were constructed. Few people gathered on the village green for the funeral; the fear of cholera infected the bonds of friendship.

Only Mildred walked with the families behind the straining horse as it dragged its load of dead up the lane. She sat among the weeping women and children as William led a service of commemoration. The painted ceiling arched above the quick and the dead.

'You're limping again, Millie,' said William.

They were in the parlour after the funeral service, too exhausted to drink the glasses of Madeira that Rose had brought.

He looked as miserable as she felt.

'A stone in my shoe, it's nothing,' she lied. She sipped the wine he had given her. 'It was a wonderful moving service, William. I'm sure it brought great comfort. It's so terribly sad. What will the women do now they have lost their men? What can we do to help?'

William rested his head in his hands. 'I fear for them too, raising children with no husbands. We must keep them from the workhouse.'

'There's still sewing work needed to make the church kneelers. If any of them are good with a needle ... Perhaps Thomas could do with some help in the kitchen garden? It's not much ...'

'We must be grateful, at least, that there are no new cases of cholera, Millie.'

She was glad he didn't mention her limp again. Over the past year, it was something she had hidden from him; the pains in her hip and knees which had gradually become more severe. Stiff in the morning when she rose, sore in the day when she walked, she wondered if these physical problems were going to make painting the rest of the church ceiling impossible. How would she climb the ladder with stiff sore knees? Or even pull on the trousers that she painted in each day?

Mildred could not admit she was suffering for if she did he

would not let her paint. She could not discuss it with the doctor either. How infuriating that the doctor considered her health was William's business! She had no other option but to try the treatments sold by a travelling herbalist. The white willow bark made a bitter tea which made her retch but she drank it in the hope that it might ease her pains.

'You're going to paint the rest of the church?' Ann asked.

Mildred and William were visiting the Owens. The women sat on a garden swing watching the men toss balls for the girls. There was laughter and teasing as catches were made or balls dropped.

'Yes, the ceiling above the nave,' said Mildred.

'And William's agreed?'

'Not without a bit of a battle as you can imagine! But yes, he sees that it is necessary.'

'And Edward? Is he involved, too?' Ann's tone could not disguise her feelings of dislike.

Mildred said: 'Edward, yes, he was keen I should do it.'

'Because he doesn't have to do the work. That man! It's quite easy to encourage someone *else* to stand in the cold and the dark for months on end, Mildred.'

Mildred was amused. 'You don't like him, do you Ann? Edward is now far too busy with commissions in London to spend his time here in Suffolk. As we know, he's an ambitious man, determined to make his mark. Keen to take any work – if it's in London.'

'Better than the backwaters of East Anglia? Let's hope the Bishop does not find out he's losing his man,' said Ann pointedly. Helen was asleep in the perambulator. Ann pushed the buggy over to a shadier area near the canary cage. 'My pretty ones,' she cooed.

Mildred followed: 'I know you didn't trust him, Ann. But I was never in any danger, I can assure you of that. I *needed* Edward Blackburne at the time. His advice and experience, perhaps his interest even, to do what I wanted to do. He helped me a great deal in the beginning.'

William was rummaging in the bushes, presumably for a ball which was lost. He found it and catching sight of her, waved it triumphantly, a big smile on his face, his hair flailing in the breeze.

'Perhaps he was in love with me, I don't know. You may have been right, Ann. All I know is that I don't need Edward now. I know what I am doing ...'

'It's very important to you, isn't it, this ceiling? What drives you to climb up to that great height in the freezing cold, to persuade your doubtful husband, face the suspicions of locals and cynics and gossips, all so that you could paint a ceiling? You couldn't even depend on me, your friend – I tried to stop you! Yet you battle on, determined to succeed. Why?'

Ann looked at her curiously. It was a look that did not demand an explanation so much as for Mildred to be truthful with herself. Later, she wondered why it was then, on that particular day, that she decided to reveal her secret, the one she had kept from everyone in Huntingfield for so many years. Ann had shared her past; why should she, Mildred, not do the same? 'Shall we walk?'

The laughter of the girls, the singing of the canaries; there could never be a better time. Mildred said quietly: 'You've probably wondered why William and I don't have any children.

You've never asked me to explain, and for that I am grateful, Ann. But ... but ...' Mildred stopped walking.

Ann touched her sleeve. 'What is it, Mildred?'

'There was a child once. William and I had a baby; a daughter, a lovely little girl.'

Ann gasped. Mildred continued: 'She is never far from our thoughts.'

But we rarely talk about her, William and I, thought Mildred. Too agonising to put into mere words the memories of our beloved child. Why am I talking today? I find I am, and it feels oddly soothing to do so.

Mildred began to walk again; slow, steady, deliberate steps that mirrored her words. 'We were living in Lincolnshire. William had been ordained and we were newly married, enjoying our first home. William did parish work. We were excited, thrilled, when we found out that I was pregnant. Then our darling daughter was born. The happiest of days. We called her Charlotte ...'

Her throat ached and she had to persuade herself to swallow. 'One day, Charlotte became unwell, feverish. At first we were not concerned. She was a strong child, no reason why she would not recover. But after a day and a night, we realised it was not a simple cold. The doctor came. No ... You know how it goes with scarlatina fever. It works quickly, rages through the body like a terrible fire. Within a few days, Charlotte was dead. Just two years old, our daughter was no more. It was the most appalling ripping of the heart. Suddenly we were bereft, alone, our daughter gone.'

Mildred was scarcely aware they had reached the end of the garden. For a few moments, the women stood and watched Richard set up croquet hoops on the lawn while William showed the girls how to hold a mallet.

'That was more than twenty years ago, and there's still an

ache in my chest, Ann. Seared into me, the shock of that still body. After that, everything changed. It had been our intention to live in Lincolnshire, to make our life there. But I couldn't bear to stay, it reminded me too much of her. We began to think of other options. We were lucky when William's uncle, who knew of our tragedy, bought us the living in Huntingfield. When we couldn't take up the position straightaway, it was William's father who pointed out that we could live relatively cheaply abroad. We didn't think it would be for so long, but it turned out we were away for eight years.

'It was a good for us, Ann, leaving Lincolnshire and spending all that time together. I can see that now. It helped me and William to forge a new life. We found out different things about each other, a new way of being.'

Her voice was almost a whisper.

'We always hoped for another child. But it's never happened. We went to many doctors on the Continent, clever men who said they could help. I was poked and prodded, given treatment, tisanes, medicines. I went to a hypnotist, a clairvoyant, a quack. Nothing worked. It's my fault, Ann, it must be. I have denied William the chance of having more children! And yet he forgives me. He forgives me every day ...'

Helen had woken from her nap; they could hear the baby whimpering. Ann looked questioningly at Mildred who nodded, and the woman fetched the crying child. Mildred watched Ann as she soothed her baby, held her, comforted her. Helen patted her mother's face, pushed her fingers into her mother's mouth. Mildred's heart lurched with the agony of a love she keenly missed.

'I sometimes wonder what Charlotte would be doing if she were still alive. A young woman by now, a family of her own perhaps? When I am up there in the church, painting the angels, I feel I am with her. In some strange way, I am with my Charlotte and with the children I might have had that I will never know. It's my tribute to her, I suppose, to make the church as beautiful as she once was. And I find it helps me.'

'I understand.' Ann murmured into her child's cheek, kissing it.

'It absorbs me, being up there, so far away from everything, concentrating on my work. I lose myself. In some way it heals me. I don't think of the future or the past, I am simply there, in the moment. In some way, complete.'

Her face was as dark as a church as they drove back to Huntingfield.

'I told her everything,' was all she said to William as she climbed in the trap and she was grateful he asked nothing more, only turned the trap for home. The horse's hooves rang crisp on the metalled lane. Purple rosebay willow herb, white campion and self-heal grew along the grassy edge. Honeysuckle, tangled through the hedgerows, scented the air. An imperceptible shift in her being as though the shell that had encased her for so long had cracked. A sense of pressure relieved.

'Let's get to bed early tonight, Millie,' said William as they clattered up the Rectory drive, 'and I will stroke your feet and you will sleep.'

# 27

'Morning, John!' Over the hedge, she saw the man hoeing weeds between neat lines of vegetables. It took her a moment to realise why he looked different. But of course! He was moving about without crutches.

'Good morning to you, Mrs Holland. You've noticed. I made meself a wooden leg, so now I can gets about without the sticks. Leather man made it for me; a strap that goes round me stump and buckles to me waist. I can walk well enough as you can see.'

His gait was a peculiar lurching motion but he made it unassisted over to the path. From beneath his trouser leg there protruded a piece of wood shaped like a boot.

'Would you sit, Mrs Holland?' He indicated a bench pushed up against the cottage wall. It was pleasant to be in the sun and for a few moments, she sat and he stood by her in comfortable silence. Then she began.

'I have decided to complete the rest of the ceiling, John. To paint over the nave. It's about the same size area as I painted last time over the chancel.'

'I see. A big job then. And is Mr Blackburne, he is involved, Ma'am, as before?'

'Mr Blackburne is a busy man. He is not able to help us this time.'

'Us?'

'You will be the foreman again I trust, John? I'm depending on you. I could not do the work without you.'

'Of course I will help you, Mrs Holland, and grateful too for the work.'

'This time, I will need some additional help. You're a practical man and you're used to dealing with … difficulties. I cannot manage the climb now. I don't propose to go into any detail but I will find climbing the ladders impossible. I'd be most grateful if you would devise a way to help me ascend the scaffolding. Be inventive, John!'

She was not surprised when John accepted this request calmly. He was never ruffled by difficulties. He had overcome enough in his own life not to raise concerns when presented with practical problems. John took it all in his stride, however lop-sided that was. She had not realised quite how much she had missed having John in her life.

'Could I have a word please, Mrs Holland?'

Rose stood at the door of the studio. Mildred looked up. 'One moment, Rose.' Her tone was a little sharp; she had just started to work. 'Yes, what is it?'

'I'd like to ask permission, Ma'am.'

'Permission? To do what?' She noticed the servant was shifting about. 'Have you got fleas Rose? Do stand still!'

'No Ma'am, yes Ma'am. It's awkward, though, and I hope you don't mind.'

'Mind what?'

'I … I needs a day off.'

'Indeed, and for what reason is that? It is not easy to cope without you at the Rectory. Rose, please, look me in the face when you speak. I've told you that several times.'

'It's Owen Walton, Ma'am.' Rose peered cautiously through dark eyelashes; her expression was hard to fathom.

'And is there a problem with Walton? One of John's workmen if I'm not mistaken.'

'You are not, Ma'am.'

'I'm not what?'

'Mistaken.'

'Yes, yes indeed. Do get on with it, Rose! Why do you mention Walton?'

'He's asked me, Ma'am.'

'Asked you what?'

'To marry him.'

'To marry him? Oh Rose! Congratulations.' Mildred smiled at the girl, put down her pen. 'That is good news. Mr Holland will also be pleased to hear this. So you would like a day off?'

'So we can get married, Ma'am. A day what suits you and the Rector.'

'Yes, of course. I'll discuss it with the Rector tonight.'

Rose, in her late-thirties, the blushing bride-to-be, turned and left the room. How charming, thought Mildred and returned to her drawing.

# 28

R ose laid them out the night before. The thick stockings, undershirt, trousers and smock, her painting clothes, clean but still reeking of paint and something else she couldn't quite place. Damp, fear, a combination of both? As she plaited her curls, a thinner face looked back at Mildred, three years older than the last time she had been dressed in this outfit. She pulled the cap down over her head, tucking in strands of loose hair and drawing it tight with a drawstring and a knot. Not looking my best but only the spiders see me once I'm up there. A twist of anxiety snaked through her belly.

'I'm coming down!' she called out loudly.

This was the sign for the servants to disappear. Mildred descended the stairs on her backside, a slightly undignified way of moving but far less painful than bending at the hip and knee, particularly in the morning when her joints were stiff. Thick trousers were a godsend, she thought, as she bumped slowly down over each step; the material provided some cushioning. A quick breakfast and a hug from William, and she picked her way across the dark churchyard. The brazier was already lit and steam from a large pan wafted over the headstones. The church bell rang seven times as she pushed open the door of the church. Inside the familiar sight of John pottering around the church, getting things ready for the day's work.

'Good morning, John. Here we are again. This time to paint the nave.'

'Morning, Mrs Holland. Yes indeed, and looking forward to it. I've started the boiler, should feel warmer in here soon. Make it easier for you than when it were so bitter.'

'And for you, John. I know you too ended up with chilblains.' She steeled herself to look up at the scaffolding. Built from wooden poles and tied with rope, it formed three levels. Owen Walton, Rose's husband was at the top, nailing panelling between the roof beams. The couple had married in the church a few weeks ago, followed by a wedding breakfast in the tavern. William had settled the bill.

Above Owen, all Mildred could see was a white expanse of boarded ceiling; no colour, no angels.

'No fool's gold,' she teased herself. Turning back to John, she said: 'I told you, John, I cannot manage to climb the ladders this time.'

Puffs of vapour spiralled around John's mouth as he explained. 'I've fashioned a sling from thick webbing and laced in leather straps. You must sit in the sling and be winched up the scaffolding.'

She gazed suspiciously at the pulley fixed to a wooden pole high above her.

'It's strong enough, Mrs Holland,' John went on. 'The leather man stitched it as well as he did the strap for me crutches. We've tested it with men double your weight.'

'Of course, John, of course you have.' Mildred smiled brightly, hoping she looked more confident than she felt. 'We may as well start.'

There was nothing for it but to give herself up to the strength of two men as they winched her up on the rope. Each pull caused a sickening lurch. She felt herself fly up several feet each time, then swing about, feet dangling, until the other man took over. Mildred gripped the sides of the webbing, fighting the temptation to look down. She tried to think about how quickly the air temperature dropped as the ground receded. She shivered from a combination of cold and fear. This time will be better than three years ago, she told herself. At least I know what I am doing.

Reaching the first platform took barely half a minute. One of the other workmen was waiting there to catch her, to swing her over to the platform and then to aid her ungainly struggle on to her feet. Then she must take another sling up to the higher-level platform. And so the process was repeated until she had reached the top.

Mildred clung to the poles of the scaffolding's frame to study her canvas; over thirty wooden panels fixed between the curving rafters. For the first time in many months, she felt a rush of excitement.

'Millie, are you all right? How was the journey up?' She looked down to see William beaming up.

'It's worked very well,' she shouted back. 'A bit unfamiliar, of course, swinging about like a bird on a breeze.'

'You'll start today?'

'The preparatory work's almost done, so yes.'

'Good luck then, dear! I shall see you for tea.'

She studied her 'painting bed'. It was John's suggestion. When lying on it flat on her back, the bed would hold her some eighteen inches from the ceiling. It would mean she could paint lying down in relative comfort. The bed also had wheels so it could be moved to a new position and then be secured with blocks. Climbing on to it, she wrenched her hip. The pain made her gasp and she lay back gratefully until the throbbing eased.

As long as she resisted the urge to look down, she told herself, she might be resting in her bed. Walton came back up the ladder with bed warmers. She nodded and he tucked them around her, and then laid a blanket over her. Lighting the lamps John had fixed to the bed and hooking her artist's box to the bed's post, he looked at her.

'Thank you, Walton, I have everything I need now.' Did he flush as she said his name?

She pulled on thin fingerless gloves, the second pair that Elizabeth had made for her. Good luck gloves, Mildred smiled. Soft and pliant, they'd soon be stiffened with paint. She dug in her pocket for a pencil. It all felt wonderfully familiar, this stretching up to apply the soft lead to plaster. She was glad to be here again. Her eyes traced the vast gulf of white expanse above her and across to the far side of the church. Perhaps they were right, whoever it was that started that rumour, that she was mad? She looked over at the ceiling she'd previously painted. Happily insane then, if that was what drove her to paint! For where once a plain brown hammer beam roof spanned the church, now proud golden angels ruled, surrounded by a tapestry of colour.

She considered her plans. In this part of the church, there would be twelve male saints portrayed in two forms; as men on the lower panel and as heavenly figures in the upper part. Each would carry the religious symbol with which he was most closely associated: Peter the Keys of Heaven, Andrew with the Cross and so on.

But today she would begin with one of the two female figures to complete the fresco: Margaret of Antioch. The patron saint of childbirth, Margaret honoured women going through the agonies of labour and delivery. Mildred had been looking forward to painting her favourite saint. For Margaret would understand that Mildred too was going through a labour, giving birth to something that was beautiful. Perhaps not as beautiful as a living child, not as beautiful as Charlotte had been when she was alive or even when dead, lying in that small casket, cold and still; but still a beauty that was worth the agony of delivery. And as Mildred drew, she began to pray, prayers for her dead child and for the loneliness that only the mothers of children who have died can truly appreciate. That after the agony of labour and delivery, the pain of memory.

Rose put her postcard of Margate and the little pot that Mrs Holland had given her into a basket. It was the first time she'd been back to her room since her marriage. She was a wife now, different from the girl who had walked up the aisle of St Mary's. She was a woman, and knew the pleasures of the marital bed. Her sister had warned her that 'it' was an unfortunate consequence of married life, something men wanted and women dutifully accepted. But she, Rose, had enjoyed it all very much indeed.

Rose stretched herself out along the counterpane, didn't even slip her shoes off, and thought with relish over the last few months. She had always dreamed that one day she would be married and now she was: Mrs Owen Walton. Owen would make a good husband, of that she was sure. Born in Huntingfield, same as she was, somehow she had never noticed the boy with the face pocked from measles or the short quiet man he'd become. Not until he was working with John at the church, that is. Owen had knocked at the back door of the house one day to collect fresh milk for Mrs Holland's tea. He and Rose had got talking; unusual as neither of them said much. The weather or the harvest or some such subject, she couldn't remember which. After that, it seemed that most days Owen found an excuse to come to the house and Rose knew she waited for his knock on the door. They got to know each other. He said she was lovely, just the way she was; no one had ever said that to her before.

So even if Owen was not the most handsome man in the village, Rose was happy. He was well thought of, Mr Holland had said so when he had married them; brave and trustworthy. He'd helped to save the church from that fire. It made Rose hum with pride when that was said and walking back down the church, everyone knew her husband was a man who deserved respect.

Rose didn't like to remember the church fire. They were good people, the Hollands; she couldn't be more grateful. They had decided not to prosecute Mary; instead they paid for the doctor to give her some calming medication and bought her a piglet so she could start raising one again for meat. Mary was coping better now. Rose just prayed that that husband of hers didn't come back to the village and get her pregnant again. Seth was nothing like her Owen, she hummed. And now he was John's regular worker, Owen might have steady employment for several years yet. Enough to support a family, Rose thought wistfully.

# 29

1865 SPRING

'It's been over two years now, and still the church is not open.' Judy adjusted the shawl around her shoulders with an impatient shake. 'Why is it taking so long? It's terrible, that the village can't worship in their own church and have to go to another parish. They're a strange lot at Cookley, I hear.'

It was a Sunday in late September. Rose set some wild roses and a spray of golden flag in a little vase by Judy's bed.

'Mrs Holland is up there most every day, working away. Here let me shake your pillows, Judy. And I've brought you a slice of chicken. I've saved it from my luncheon.'

Carefully she unfolded a white cloth to reveal some pieces of chicken breast.

Judy sniffed suspiciously. 'Very nice, I'm sure. Chicken. When did I last have a piece of meat? And "luncheon" you call it. Very grand.' Her tone was mocking but she looked greedily at the meat. 'You've started using strange words since your wedding, Mrs Walton. But remember, Owen is only a labourer and once that work at the Rectory stops, who knows?'

She frowned at Rose.

'I'll have that chicken for my supper. Give it to Ned when you leave. So why is the work in the church taking so long? The last time it took her no more than ...?'

'About six months. But she says these paintings are more hard to do.'

Judy gave her a sceptical look.

'Of course, when I take her the draft drawings, I can see that for meself.'

'Very much the expert now, are we?'

'There's no Mr Blackburne no more. Haven't seen him at the Rectory for ages. Not since that day, a few years ago it must be now, when he left the Rectory so quick. I told you about that, didn't I?'

'No doubt you did, you're always one to rattle on. Go on then. I'll have that piece of chicken now,' said Judy.

She picked delicately at the pieces of flesh, patting with a handkerchief after each mouthful. 'Delicious, that will help me to get better. Now where were we? Ah yes. I did hear from one of the worker's wives that Mrs Holland is winched up the scaffold, Rose, rather than climbing the ladder. Now why would that be?' She looked suspiciously at Rose, sensing there might be a piece of information she needed.

Rose knew why she had never told Judy about Mildred's arthritis, her difficulty with dressing, how she winced when she moved. A sense of loyalty. It was not discussed among the other servants either as though everyone agreed it was a secret. When Mildred called out that she was coming downstairs, they all pretended they had something to do and hurried away to another part of the house. They acted as though they could not hear Mildred riding the stairs like a child on a sledge.

A string of chicken flesh hung from Judy's lip. 'Why is she being winched up the scaffold?' she repeated.

'There's something left on your lip,' said Rose and watched

as Judy's tongue flicked out to catch the piece of meat. 'Less tiring than climbing,' she said.

Some days Mildred was confined to bed with pain. She would ask for her meals in the bedroom, cups of special tea for her headaches and fresh chillies to nibble; some people said chillies were good for arthritis. And the laudanum which she finally persuaded the doctor to give her; the physician had agreed not to tell William. Sometimes it gave her nightmares. One night, she dreamed she was painting the figure of a saint on the ceiling but when she stretched out to apply colour to the face, it was Edward who looked back at her. His dark eyes accused her and he mouthed words she could not understand.

She woke with a shudder. It must be almost five years since they had last met. With the thinnest veneer of politeness, she had banished Edward from her presence for daring to link himself with her work, her painting! Yet now, with the distance of time, she could acknowledge how much she had relied on him. He had been invaluable, patient in his own way, and kind.

Another time she dreamed she was being winched up to the scaffold, swinging through the clean, cold air. But it was James who reached out to catch her in the sling and pull her towards him. A hot rush of desire engulfed her and she woke suddenly, her body tingling with the memory of his touch. She remembered how much he had helped her too but in a different way, touched without sensation a part of her that had been lying dormant. He would be a grown man now. It was more than ten years since she had seen him. The last they heard from his father Sydney was that James was working for a teak company in Burma. She smiled to know the boy had defied his father after all.

William always prayed for her, asking God to keep her safe and well. But by the third year of her painting the nave, his prayers became petitions. Doubts about her health preoccupied him. He genuinely feared that she would not be able to complete the task that she had set herself. Each week, it was becoming more difficult for her to move. He knew she was uncomfortable about him seeing her so sore and stiff, even if she was never explicit. Her ill health was never mentioned. So in the morning, he always professed a compelling hunger for breakfast and left the bedroom quickly, leaving her to struggle down from the bed without him there to witness how painful it was for her to reach for the floor put on her stockings or tie her laces. If she said she was staying in bed for the day, it was spoken of as though she had succumbed to a recent change in the weather. It was never acknowledged it was her arthritis. But it was obvious from the way she buttered her bread, shuffled along the corridor or always sat in a high-backed chair how affected she was.

That winter, he suggested they take a holiday somewhere hot and return to Huntingfield in the spring. But she had dismissed this idea with a weary wave. She was far too busy for holidays! She must finish painting the ceiling. Mildred was never one to make a fuss or to complain, he admired her for that, but pain was etched across her face. His wife was ageing quickly and working slowly.

He took to visiting the church during the day. He would slip in, gesturing to John to keep his presence unknown, and find a spot where he could observe the changing landscape of the ceiling. It was marvellous to witness saints spilling out from her brush or to watch a plain border become a fairground frieze of rosettes, stripes and dots. Other days, he would call out to say he had come to see her. He would sit under the east window and sing her hymns or practise his sermon.

He had never been up on the scaffolding himself. Only once had he asked if he might join her there. Her mouth said 'yes' but her eyes said 'please don't'. In some way, he was relieved. He accepted that the scaffold was her private place up near the angels, a space she preferred to keep as her own.

So from the ground he watched as the chancel roof was gradually covered with images and colour. Then the second groups of angels, garments speckled with stars and flowers, gold crowns and wings, shields held aloft, were settled into their positions, leaping from the roof beams, frozen in glory. On Sunday, he told Mildred as they drove to Cookley (she had become too slow to walk over the hill) that he would tell the congregation the church would open next month.

It was waiting for her in the parlour. A big rectangular box tied with string sat under the window. A man from the Heveningham estate had brought it, Rose told her.

'What is it?' Mildred was delighted. 'It's not my birthday.'

'Nothing to do with me.' William was reading his post. He looked up and smiled. 'Something you ordered from London, no doubt. I've asked Thomas to bring tools to open it.'

'It's very heavy,' she said as she tried to manoeuvre the box. She started to pick at the paper that wrapped it. Then Thomas cut the binding and wrenched out the nails securing the lid. A box full of sawdust. Fingers burrowed urgently into the dry shavings and she felt something solid.

'Here, lift it out, Thomas! Be careful.'

Struggling with its weight, like a phoenix from the ashes, Thomas lifted out a stained glass window, about four feet high and three feet wide, encased in a wooden frame. It showed a haloed Virgin Mary standing on a crescent moon, her hands crossed at the chest. She was set within a cloud-filled oval filled with tiny squares of shimmering purple.

'Oh, William, look at this! Do help Thomas take it to the window.'

Now sunlight streamed through the deep blue of the Virgin's robes and her cascading yellow curls. It picked out tiny painted details on the Virgin's feet and face and a thin line of glowing green glass.

'It's stunning! But who made it? Surely it's not from ...?' The familiar handwriting on a card confirmed it was.

'I'd rather forgotten,' said William. 'Ann wrote to ask for the measurements for the window about six months ago. Did wonder if she'd get round to it. Quite charming. Made for the south aisle, Millie.'

'And Richard? What did he say?'

'Richard was keen that she should do it.'

The card read:

*To the glory of God and to celebrate the completion of St Mary's renovation. With love from Richard and Ann Owen.*

# 30

1866 SPRING

When she first moved to Huntingfield, she had spent many hours at her bedroom window looking out over the heads of the seven Irish yew trees that stood by the Rectory like brooding monsters. The countryside had frightened her. But after twenty years, she had grown to love what had once made her feel unsettled. Now it sustained her. The turn and twist of the land as it rose and sank, the creaking trees, the lingering green gentle on her tight-wound eyes. She was grateful, almost greedy to acknowledge her inconsequentiality in the greater scheme of nature.

And the drawing, the painting, the gilding, it is complete. No longer does she rise each day through the cold stone building, dangling on the end of a rope. Over 250 books of gold leaf glisten on the tips of angel wings and highlight the halos of saints. Frescos cover the ceiling of St Mary's and angels proudly grace the church. Her brushes and paints are cleaned and put away. The ugly spindles of scaffolding have been dismantled and the paraphernalia of building has vanished. The simple space has been swept clean and the wooden pews carried back to their rightful rows. Working boots no longer tramp the tiles.

When the doors of the church open once again to welcome the congregation, they will see the work is done.

On William's insistence, she sends to London for a new dress and coat and hat. She must look her fashionable best, he says. New vestments are ordered for William too; a white and gold satin robe in which he will take the service. Boxes arrive: a new Bible for the lectern, a thurible on a long gold chain in which fragrant spices are burned to create perfumed smoke, two enormous candlesticks for the altar and a gold cup and bowl for the Communion wine and bread. New hymn books and kneelers are set at each pew and, and while Rose gives the place a final dust, Walton cuts the churchyard grass. Next Sunday, the church will open again.

Then William gives her a letter.

He had kept it as a surprise. So she was shocked to read that Sydney and James would be 'delighted to attend the church opening and grateful for the invitation to spend the weekend at the Rectory'.

'James and Sydney staying here?' Her heart thumped uncomfortably but she was also excited at the prospect. 'In three days' time! Have you warned Cook?'

'You are pleased, my dear?' William examined her face carefully. 'Yes, I told her we will have two guests coming to stay, and Rose is preparing the guest rooms. But I regard the Peglers as such good friends that there's no need to make a great fuss, do you agree?' He stroked her cheek. 'I want the opening to be special for you, Millie.'

'So James is back in England?'

'On a visit, I understand. He gets leave from the company every two years.'

On Saturday morning she was nonplussed to see two cart loads piled with flowers and greenery coming up the Rectory drive. Rose ran in with a message for William. They were sent by Lady

Huntingfield with her compliments for the opening of the church. There was no time to be lost, they must be arranged. 'Rose, help me dress quickly.' Mildred stood by the mirror while the woman closed the line of tiny silk buttons of a green spotted jacket. It had arrived from London along with a matching pleated silk skirt and hat. They said that in London the fashion was for narrow skirts and Tyrolean-style hats; this outfit was clearly following the trend.

'I shall miss you Rose, when you leave.' How nervy Mildred felt today. 'Thank you for staying on to help with the opening of the church. I do appreciate it.'

'I'm only pregnant, Ma'am,' said Rose. 'My mother worked up until the day she laboured, and was back the next.'

'You have Walton to look after you now and you must start to rest. Here, Rose, I've been meaning to give this to you ever since you told me about the baby. I know you've always liked it.'

Into Rose's palm Mildred placed the little amber brooch which William had bought her in Southwold. He agreed she should give it to Rose; the Southwold visit held strange memories for them both.

'Oh Ma'am, it's the most lovely thing I've ever had.' Pieces of amber formed a butterfly-shaped brooch. She slipped it into her apron. 'Thank you for it. I shall always treasure it.'

Rose finished pinning Mildred's hair and perched the peaked hat on the front of the curls.

'What time are the Peglers expected today, Ma'am?'

'This afternoon. In case they haven't eaten lunch, ask Cook to set out some cold meats and bread in the dining room, will you please?'

Mildred studied herself in the mirror. How much had she aged since she had last seen James? Her face was thinner, a little drawn perhaps and dark patches haunted her eyes, but her hair had kept its colour and her teeth were good. William said she was still beautiful. She shrugged and limped over to the staircase, lowering herself gingerly down each step using only her right leg; the hip was less painful on that side.

Outside, it was warm and still. She followed the path across the graveyard between the headstones and pushed open the heavy door. A heady waft of perfume hit her. Roses, honeysuckle, phlox, jasmine and sweet peas stood in bowls, their scent filling the church. Tiny bouquets of bay, rosemary and thyme tied with ribbon to each pew. Two tall vases of white arching lilies were set on the altar. Looking down on it all, their calm unchanging faces, were her golden angels. Mildred gazed around with a mixture of relief, thanks and deep sadness. Seven years ago, this church had been forlorn and neglected. Today it was known and cared for. Tomorrow it would be offered to the congregation of Huntingfield and to God. She said a prayer for all who would worship there and for those she would never meet.

Why was she surprised by the streaks of grey in his hair, his thickened waist and his sun-stained skin? She had not seen James for over ten years and he had spent a good deal of it in the tropical sun. But his direct gaze remained untouched by time and as he bent to kiss her hand in welcome, she remembered his long, pale fingers. She was very pleased to see him and even more relieved to realise that whatever hold he may have had over her had dissipated like mist.

'James! How wonderful to see you. And Sydney, so kind of you to have come all this way to see us. Please come in, both of you!'

I wonder if they find me changed too, she thought, as she led her guests to the dining room, glad the bustle on her dress might hide her limp.

It was a happy party that afternoon. They ate and drank and caught up on family news. Philip the elder boy had won a seat in Parliament and given a successful maiden speech. James had just been appointed to a new position with a company exporting oil from Upper Burma to Europe. He also had personal news.

'I plan to marry. My fiancée is called Amelia, Amelia Goodley. She was born in India, where her father was in the diplomatic service, so she knows the difficulties of living in the colonies. She was schooled in Surrey where she still lives with an aunt. Actually I have my father to thank for the introduction.' He nodded in deference to Sydney.

'Another Oxford connection, William. You remember Cecil Goodley?'

'This is very good news, James! No, terrible memory I have, not sure I do recall him.'

'Amelia and I hope to marry before I return to Burma next month. Then she will join me there as soon as a passage can be arranged.'

Mildred was genuinely happy to congratulate James.

'This is very good news. I long to meet your Amelia and hope I shall someday soon. Now James, have you finished? I want to show you my studio. Sydney, you'd prefer to stay here? This way, James!'

They left William and Sydney discussing Oxford days as they crossed the yard to the studio.

'So things are working out well for you, James? And you've shown your father that you could make your own way. He seems content with your position.'

'He has forgiven me, at last, for not going into the Church. And we get on much better since I have lived abroad. I write often. We have found a way to accept each other. And he is happy now to have found me a wife.'

They stood in the studio. Light picked out the dust motes which danced on the breeze from a broken pane. Scrolls of paper rustled on the long table. He looked at her and she nodded. He stretched out one of the drawings. It was of the white pelican, her long curled neck pecking at her breast, drawing out her blood, sacrificing herself in order to feed her young brood. She remembered the serious way he had of considering her work, the careful time he took to examine each part.

'So you found it, the courage to do it.'

'I did.'

'And tomorrow, I will see it.'

'Tomorrow you will see if I have achieved it; tomorrow, when the church opens.'

# 31

1866 THE NEXT DAY

I cannot go today, Mildred whispers to William at daybreak. She has slept so little and she is in too much pain to rise from the bed and to dress and to attend the service. She is content that people in the village will come to worship and to see it for themselves. But she will not be with them. Her knees and hips throb with swelling. She fights back tears.

There is another reason she must linger in the bed. She cannot be there when they come to judge her. She remembers now the first time, how upset she was, seared raw by the inquisitive upturned faces, desperate to read from their expressions what they thought. She cannot go through it again. It was too raw, too personal; her feelings, hopes, dreams, laid out across the ceiling for all to see. William kisses her gently and leaves. She reaches for the laudanum and she falls into a dreamless sleep.

She is woken by William's voice booming up from the hallway. He is calling everyone together to leave for church: Sydney, James, Rose, Thomas, Cook. The clunk as the front door closes and the household noises still. Faint sounds of people's voices, children calling and horses' hooves on the lane drift over as she rests back against the pillows. Organ music sends her to sleep again.

Sometime later she is woken again by voices in the churchyard. The service must be over. She feels compelled to see who has been to see the decorated church. She chivvies herself out of bed. The church cannot be seen from her bedroom window. She hobbles over to the stairs and begins to crawl on her hands and knees up to the attic floor. She pulls herself upright and stands for a moment, catching her breath. Pain flames at the hip, but memory also pricks. The last time she stood here, the new mistress of the Rectory, she found the nursery and Rose found her, weeping on the floor. She has not been back up here since then. The nursery has remained unused, abandoned, for over twenty years.

No wonder then that the door is stuck. She gives it a shove and it creaks open. As rusty as I am, she thinks. The room is as she remembered, bare except for a bench and tatty curtains. She limps over to the window and peers through the dust-smeared glass into the churchyard. She sees the path packed with villagers milling about, pleased to be outside on a lovely day, men, women and children in their Sunday best. Some she recognises and others she does not. Can she tell from looking at them, the way they move and stand, what they think of the ceiling, of the renovations? Do they like what they have seen?

Then it comes to her as a revelation and a relief. She does not mind what they think. The act of painting allowed her to express herself; her feelings of bereavement and her love of God and beauty. Let others judge her and if she is found wanting, then so be it. She is not the finest of artists but she is a brave and committed one. And that, for her, must be sufficient.

William is by the church door, shaking hands, exchanging words with the people as they leave. There is Ann, splendid in a large brown hat and coat, and Richard. What does she think of her gift to the church which now graces the south aisle? With them Sarah, Grace and Helen, accomplished young women who nod at acquaintances and guide their parents smoothly through the crowd.

Then she has a shock. For she was not expecting to see Edward Blackburne. He shakes William's hand energetically, shares a few words, perhaps asks where she is, and then greets the Pegler men who stand to one side. She can deny it to herself no more; how much she owes Edward. It was not fair to be so angry with him. If I cannot see him today, I will write and thank him. He bows to Ann and Richard before disappearing out of the gate.

And now there is John Hammant with his wife and daughters. Even from so far away, she can see the girls' carefully plaited hair and clean shoes. John should be proud, she thinks, of all that he has done in the renovation of St Mary's. He shakes hands with William and then the family makes it way down the path to the wheeled chair left by the gate.

Mr Edwards the tailor and his diminutive wife nod to William; Mildred remembers how awkward she felt when being measured up for trousers. The man who runs the post office, his name has escaped her, shakes William's hand, and then Thomas walks by with his father. In the crowd she can see Cook and Hal the shepherd. All these people have played some part in my life over the past ten years. We are misguided to think we achieve anything alone.

She is just about to return to bed when she catches sight of someone else leaving the church, someone in a wheeled chair. She presses up close against the window to see who is swaddled in that thick shawl, a squashy hat pulled down low over the face. A similar chair to the one that John made; she was not aware of another being used in the village. And then the person turns her head. Mildred gasps. Judy Scott! Judy, who has not left her bed in thirty years, is in St Mary's churchyard being pushed along the path by Owen Walton. Rose is close behind, helping Ned to shuffle duck-like after his wife. Judy's head swivels from side to side like a pendulum; the long nose and white cheeks appear and disappear with each turn. How strange it must be after so many years living inside to feel the fresh air on your skin, to smell the damp earth and to see the sky above your head!

Then Judy makes a gesture and Owen stops pushing the chair. Judy slowly turns her head again, but this time far enough around that her gaze carries over her right shoulder and up to the Rectory. She lifts her eyes and stares full face at the attic window. Mildred is caught unawares. Can the woman see her? For a moment, everything is still. Then Judy raises her hand as though in acknowledgement and with a nod, the chair rumbles on down the path and out on to the lane back towards the village.

# AFTERWORD

On January 1st 2011, I visited St Mary's Church in Huntingfield with my husband. The sun was bright but inside the bitterly cold church it was gloomy until we slipped a pound coin into the meter on the wall. There was an explosion. Where above our heads the ceiling had been dark, it now shouted with wild colours and myriad images. Glorious carved golden angels leapt out from the roof beam ends. A leaflet explained that in the 1850s, Mildred Holland, the parish vicar's wife, had single-handedly created this display of religious iconography. It was bewildering. Why would a woman clamber up sixty feet without the benefits of heat or lighting to spend six years creating a 15th-century ceiling? My research revealed limited information beyond establishing the church had been white-washed in the 1580s; an invoice showed that William, Mildred's husband, had paid for the cost of paint and gold leaf; Mildred became 'crippled' in later life and the couple had no children.

It was obvious Mildred's story was waiting to be told. I hope I have done it justice.

# A NOTE FROM THE AUTHOR

Many books and other papers were used in background research for this book and I am indebted, in particular, to: *The Parson and the Victorian Parish* by Peter Hammond (1977); Huntingfield Parish Records; Mitchell Beazle's *Victorian Diaries* (2001); Sharron Marcus's *Between women: friendship, desire and marriage in Victorian England* (2007); *The Angel out of the House: Philanthropy and Gender* (2002) by Dorice Williams Elliott, *Feminism and Family planning in Victorian England* (1964) by JA Banks; *The Builder Magazine Vol 54* 1888; Edward Blackburne's *The History of Decorative Art* (1847); *Victorian Diaries: The Daily Lives of Victorian Men and Women* (2001) by Heather J. Creaton; *Biography of a Victorian Village*, Richard Cobbold's 1978 account of Wortham, Suffolk 1860 edited by Ronald Fletcher; *The Wall Paintings Workshop cleaning and conservation report on St Mary the Virgin*, Huntingfield (2006); *The Other World: Spiritualism and Psychic Research in England 1850–1914* by Janet Oppenheim; *Witches' Ladder: the hidden history* by Chris Wingfield, researcher 'The Other Within' project Pitt Rivers Museum; *The Oxford Book of Wild Flowers* by B. B. Nicholson, S. Ary and M. Gregory.

I am grateful to the staff of the British Library and the RIBA library for their kind and helpful support.

*The Huntingfield Paintress* is a work of fiction.

## ACKNOWLEDGEMENTS

If Margaret King had not suggested on New Year's Day 2011 that I visit St Mary's Church, I would never have been inspired by Mildred, so many thanks to her and Peter Berry for their encouragement. Felicity Griffin, Hannah Mills, Rachel Griffiths, Hugh Constant, Nicola O'Connoll, Alan Burnet, Caroline Oakley, Simon Chandler, Jennifer Collieson, Shalini Rao and Simon Garfield were helpful in different ways. I am grateful to Annie Ablett and John Renner for technical advice, John and Janet Murphy for the visit to Holland House and Christine Cooper for the joys of Laundry Cottage. Laura Morris, my agent, always believed Mildred deserved this tribute and Matthew Smith's energy made it happen. Many thanks to the team at Bloodhound Books for their support. Thanks and love to my sons Callum and Dylan Holmes Williams and my husband Kipper Williams.

# A NOTE FROM THE PUBLISHER

**Thank you for reading this book.** If you enjoyed it please do consider leaving a review on Amazon to help others find it too.

**We hate typos.** All of our books have been rigorously edited and proofread, but sometimes mistakes do slip through. If you have spotted a typo, please do let us know and we can get it amended within hours.

info@bloodhoundbooks.com

## PRAISE FOR THE AUTHOR

'A genuinely original, utterly enchanting story'
  –A.N.Wilson

~

'Clever, finely chiselled and immaculately observed, this rich and characterful novel superbly imagines the earthy, elemental world of Victorian England and the sizzling soap opera of village life. Love, death, artistic enterprise ... what more do you want?'
  –Mark Ellen

~

'A slice of Suffolk history brought beautifully to life'
  – Esther Freud

~

'An atmospheric and enjoyable story of a singular and free-thinking woman'

*Praise for the Author*

– Deborah Moggach

## ABOUT THE AUTHOR

Pamela Holmes was born in Charleston, South Carolina. At the age of eight, she moved with her family to England. She has two sons and lives in Somerset with her husband.

Printed in Great Britain
by Amazon

87394782R00140